W9-AFZ-232

## WHO LET THE DOG OUT?

"With his sharp wit and skillful courtroom tactics, lawyer Andy Carpenter continues to shine in *Who Let the Dog Out?* . . . Readers familiar with Andy Carpenter mysteries will discover that Rosenfelt has a solid formula, and the end result is like eating ice cream on a hot day—satisfying to the very end." —Associated Press

## HOUNDED

"David Rosenfelt deftly works in wry humor, a love of dogs, and New Jersey gangsters in *Hounded*, his highly entertaining twelfth legal thriller featuring attorney Andy Carpenter. . . . [Rosenfelt] continues to explore Andy's personality, allowing him to change and grow in each novel. Scenes in which Andy and Ricky bond are heartwarming and realistic, yet they don't detract from the complex plot. Andy's sideline of rescuing dogs to find them permanent homes—which the author shares with his character—never overwhelms the story."
—Associated Press

"Heartwarming . . . This is an entertaining, feel-good read, populated with Jersey gangsters, ruthless criminals, and likable protagonists. Longtime fans and new readers alike will be charmed by wise-cracking, canine-loving Andy."
—*Publishers Weekly*

"*Hounded* [is] great summer entertainment, a page-turning mystery with a lot of good laughs along the way."
—*Portland Press Herald*

## UNLEASHED

"Terrific . . . How does Rosenfelt manage to construct such clever and complex plots, tie them all together, make you love Andy more with every novel, and bombard you with nonstop humor, all at the same time? Only Rosenfelt can pull off that kind of quadruple-play. His is an absolutely unique mystery/comedy talent. Do not miss *Unleashed*. Don't miss any of them."          —Examiner.com

"Rosenfelt keeps readers guessing to the very end . . . [readers] will have a good time trying to solve a well-constructed puzzle."          —Associated Press

"Rosenfelt demonstrates again that he's a master storyteller in this immensely enjoyable new Andy Carpenter novel. His writing is crisp, his plot unfolds at a rapid clip, and his characters are people you'd like to hang out with. Surprises in the plot and gripping courtroom scenes make it difficult to put down."

—*RT Book Reviews* (four stars)

"A fun read. Andy is still a joke-a-page lawyer."

—*The Daily News* (Memphis)

## LEADER OF THE PACK

"A book full of excitement and action, and [a] book that will make you laugh. Out loud."          —Examiner.com

"Entertaining . . . Well-worked action scenes and fiery courtroom clashes [add] up to a good-natured read that isn't quite as easygoing as it seems. Like its hero."          —*Booklist*

"Rosenfelt still weaves a compelling narrative that will stump even the expert Perry Mason fan." —Associated Press

"A fun mystery . . . surprising enough that I gasped in public . . . The ending is deeply satisfying."
—*The Star-Ledger* (Newark)

"Andy is as effervescent as ever, and the courtroom byplay is consistently entertaining." —*Kirkus Reviews*

"Rosenfelt walks a line between pulse-pounding suspense and laugh-out-loud humor. . . . One of the best in the business. —Associated Press

# THE TWELVE DOGS
# OF CHRISTMAS

## ALSO BY DAVID ROSENFELT

# THE
# TWELVE DOGS
## OF CHRISTMAS

*David Rosenfelt*

MINOTAUR BOOKS
NEW YORK

THE TWELVE DOGS OF CHRISTMAS. Copyright © 2016 by Tara Productions, Inc. All rights reserved. Printed in the United States of America. For information, address St. Martin's Press, 175 Fifth Avenue, New York, N.Y. 10010.

www.minotaurbooks.com

The Library of Congress has cataloged the hardcover edition as follows:

Names: Rosenfelt, David, author.
Title: The Twelve dogs of Christmas : an Andy Carpenter mystery / David Rosenfelt.
Description: First Edition. | New York : Minotaur Books, 2016. | Series: An Andy Carpenter novel
Identifiers: LCCN 2016027886 | ISBN 9781250106766 (hardcover) | ISBN 9781250106773 (ebook)
Subjects: LCSH: Carpenter, Andy (Fictitious character)—Fiction. | Attorneys—Fiction. | Ex-convicts—Crimes against—Fiction. | Orphans—Fiction. | Dogs—Fiction. | BISAC: FICTION / Mystery & Detective / General. | FICTION / Suspense. | GSAFD: Suspense fiction. | Mystery fiction.
Classification: LCC PS3618.O838 T88 2016 | DDC 813/.6—dc23
LC record available at https://lccn.loc.gov/2016027886

ISBN 978-1-250-14561-1 (trade paperback)

Our books may be purchased in bulk for promotional, educational, or business use. Please contact your local bookseller or the Macmillan Corporate and Premium Sales Department at 1-800-221-7945, extension 5442, or by email at MacmillanSpecial Markets@macmillan.com.

First Minotaur Books Paperback Edition: October 2017

D   10   9   8   7   6   5   4   3

**Y**ou looking for work?"

The guy in the pickup asked the question, but he had to have already known the answer. He was at the convenience store on the edge of town where the young men hung out when they needed money and were willing to spend the day working for it.

Day laborers didn't earn much, but they didn't need much: a roof over their head, something to eat, and, more often, something to drink—that's it. And at this time of year, the roof wasn't even that necessary. So they would arrive early in the day and wait, and locals who needed to hire them would drive up and pick them out, as if from a lineup.

Chip didn't get picked much, because he was thin and pale and didn't possess the obvious physical strength of some of the others. That's why on this particular morning, on a hot July day almost two years ago, he was one of the last few left.

People called him Chip—when they bothered to call him

anything—because he had noticeable chips in his two front teeth. He never used his real name, because there was no need to. He wasn't voting or getting a credit card, a passport, or anything. He was as anonymous and untracked as one can be in the modern, data-driven world.

But no one can be completely anonymous, and no one exists that can't be tracked.

There were two of them in the front cabin of the truck, which meant that Chip had to climb onto the back. That was OK; it was over ninety degrees out, and the wind felt good in his face. He didn't know what they were hiring him to do, but he hoped it wasn't too arduous. It would be, of course; otherwise, they would do it themselves.

Chip wasn't feeling that great: his stomach had been bothering him for a couple of weeks—some shooting pains, maybe one every couple of hours—but he had no money to see a doctor. He'd heard politicians talking about universal health care, but it would have to be really universal before it found its way down to him.

The truck turned east, which told Chip that the work would be construction-related rather than agricultural. The farmland was to the west, and he was pleased that they were not going there. Chip hated farm labor, so he was happy it was obviously not in the cards for him this day.

They arrived at a construction site that looked abandoned. It was not exactly a shock that it was abandoned; there was nothing around it for miles. The site looked like it might have been the shell of a small strip mall. Maybe the people financing it walked away when they realized that building retail stores in a place where there was nobody to buy anything didn't make that much sense.

The two men got out of the truck, so Chip jumped down as well. "This is it?" Chip said.

The driver nodded. "This is it."

"What do you want me to do?"

"First things first. What's your name?"

"People call me Chip."

"I didn't ask what people call you. I asked you your name."

The question puzzled Chip, and maybe worried him a little. He hoped that this guy wasn't going to pay him by check. There was nothing Chip could do with a check. "You mean my real name?" he asked.

"Now you got it. What's your real name?"

"It doesn't matter," Chip said.

"It matters to me."

Chip had no idea why it would be of any importance, but he told the man his real name. He hadn't used it in years; he had no reason to, and it sounded somewhat strange as he said it.

What would have seemed even stranger, had Chip been able to reflect on it, was that his name coming out of his mouth would be the last words he'd ever hear.

The man from the passenger seat, who hadn't said a word, had a gun in his hand that Chip had not seen. He calmly used it to shoot Chip three times, a perfect triangle centered at the heart.

The two men calmly took the wallet off Chip's lifeless body and then lowered him into the grave that had already been dug.

They covered it over and then went back to his boarding house room, to see what else they could find and use.

**I**'m not dreaming of a white Christmas.

First of all, I almost never dream about weather, and when it comes to holidays, I'm mostly indifferent to color. Second of all, if you live in an urban environment—and Paterson, New Jersey, is as urban as it gets—snow on the streets doesn't stay white for long. It turns to brown and gray and black in no time.

But the main reason I would never dream of a white Christmas is Bing Crosby. Growing up, my mother started playing Christmas music in the house pretty much in the beginning of July, and by far the song she played most frequently was the one with Bing Crosby dreaming of that damn white Christmas, "just like the ones he used to know."

He annoyed me to the point that I researched it and found out that the Bingster grew up in Tacoma, Washington. The average snowfall in Tacoma is eight inches a year, which pretty much guarantees that the Crosby family didn't spend too many Christmases frolicking in the cold, wet stuff. White Christmases to the Crosbys were, in fact, a dream, not a reality.

I pointed this out to my mother, but she was unmoved. She said that Bing didn't have to grow up in the Arctic to be dreaming of the white stuff. Anybody could dream, she said, no matter where they lived.

When I reminded her of the crucial "just like the ones I used to know" phrase, she swatted my argument away. She said that, for all we knew, Bing could have spent his holidays visiting family in Montana or Buffalo or Iceland. According to Mom, if Crosby said it, and especially if he sang it, you could take it to the snowbank.

My mother passed away about twelve years ago, and she never did admit that Bing was lying about all those white Christmases. Of course, if you want to give him the benefit of the doubt, there's always the chance that he wasn't lying. Maybe he was reminiscing about spending his youthful Christmas holidays surrounded by Caucasians.

Christmas is still three weeks away, and when I have time I'll research it further. Right now, I'm on a case; between that and football season, there just aren't enough hours in a day.

I don't usually like to spend the preholiday period on a case. In fact, I try to work as little as possible. But the world seems always to be crying out for me, Andy Carpenter, to provide legal genius to those targeted by our justice system, and I do so more often than I'd like.

But this case is a bit different. This one I was eager to take.

**M**y client's name is Martha Boyer.

I first heard about her at least twenty years ago, and we've been sort of friends for almost fifteen. But I actually only learned her real name a few weeks ago. She never uses that name, and very few people know it.

Like everyone else, I've always thought of her as "the Puppy Lady," and when I talk to her, I call her by her chosen nickname, Pups, which is how everybody addresses her.

Pups is sixty-eight years old, another fact I learned only when I took on her case. Her husband died in a drive-by shooting in Paterson about a year and a half ago. He was leaving a restaurant with a friend and had the misfortune of being near a gang member when the shooting started. The husband, Jake Boyer, and the gang member were killed, while Boyer's friend emerged unscathed. Pups has continued to live in their house on Forty-First Street in Paterson, New Jersey, about ten blocks from me.

I'd say that about half the people who know Pups consider her cantankerous and difficult; the other half think she's a complete pain in the ass. I'm somewhere in the middle, but I can't help liking her. I think the fact that I like her pisses her off.

She doesn't much care for social niceties; it's unlikely that she spends time at fancy cocktail parties. She has a cough that is ever present, but, rather than daintily covering her mouth with a handkerchief, she turns and coughs into her shoulder and upper arm.

If she has any income, I don't know what the source is. But she seems to get by, and it never came up in our discussions about my taking on the case. I have no interest in being paid for it. I have plenty of money anyway, more than I'll ever need. And this is a worthwhile cause.

The animal shelters in Passaic County leave quite a bit to be desired. They're not as bad as shelters in some areas of the country, but that's pretty faint praise. They're overcrowded, and animals that aren't adopted can get put down. It's as simple as that, and one of the reasons why rescue groups, like the one I run with Willie Miller, help out.

Puppies, especially newborns, create a particular problem for public shelters. They need to stay there for a long while, until they are old enough to adopt out, so that uses up scant space and resources. They are also prone to disease, and shelters are a place where diseases can proliferate.

That's where Pups steps in. She takes the puppies from the shelter, along with their mothers, and she nurses and cares for them until they're ready to be placed in homes. At least that's how it started, decades ago.

For a long time now, she has been so well known that

people often bring the puppies directly to her. And if instead they bring the puppies to the shelter, the manager, Fred Brandenberger, gently advises them to take the puppies to Pups. He knows that puppies have a much better chance that way.

She never turns puppies away, so Pups's house rarely has fewer than twenty-five dogs in it. I've been there, and she keeps it amazingly clean. It's an excellent way for these dogs to come into what might otherwise have been a cold and uncaring world. As you might have guessed by now, I am a big fan of Pups.

The other thing I like about Pups is that she does not bullshit. Ever. She says exactly what's on her mind, and what's on her mind isn't always flattering. She once told me that true freedom is not caring what anyone thinks of you. She also said that she will never lie to me, and I have never doubted that even that statement was an example of her truth-telling.

Unfortunately, not everyone shares my devotion. Someone recently filed an anonymous complaint against Pups, claiming that the zoning law for the area in which she lives specifically limits the number of pets per household to three. At the time the complaint was filed, Pups was twenty-six dogs above the legal limit.

The zoning board contacted Pups about the issue, and with characteristic delicacy she suggested they "shove the complaint where the sun don't shine." The board didn't take that well and proceeded to act on the complaint. They sent Pups a notice declaring that she would have to reduce her population to three dogs or fewer or, failing that, move out. And she had thirty days to make the choice.

That's when Pups called me, asking me to represent her.

My first call was to Stanley Wade, the head of the zoning board. It's revealing of Stanley's personality that I've known him for a very long time and yet don't really have an opinion of him. He's just sort of there.

Stanley has a furniture store in real life, and his position on the zoning board is an additional thing he does on the side. He's had the job for as long as I can remember, through various mayoral changes. I doubt that he's had to fight off other contenders; it's fair to say that the position is not really coveted.

Stanley was no help at all. He basically said that the law is the law and that he simply was not empowered to change it. He made noises like he regretted the situation, without coming out and saying so. Stanley is a careful, noncontroversial man; he always speaks as if he thinks someone might be recording him.

My next move was to file suit at the county courthouse, demanding that the law be overturned or, at the very least, ignored in this case. This particular law dates back to 1881, so it has already demonstrated an excellent capacity to survive. Of course, it's never had to go up against a team as formidable as Andy Carpenter and Pups Boyer.

The suit was shuttled to Judge Irene Hough, who obviously drew the judicial short straw. In response, her initial gambit was to tell me to try and reach an amicable settlement with the zoning board. I told her that I had already made the effort but was rebuffed. She told me to risk another rebuff and try again. This was not a lawsuit she wanted tried in her courtroom.

So I dutifully went back to Stanley, who was not pleased that I had filed suit. He again refused to intervene, but this time with some annoyance mixed in with his intransigence.

I tried to reason with him. "Stanley," I said, "you really want to go into court and testify against puppies? At Christmas time? You'll get slaughtered."

Now a bit of fear entered the mix. "You can't make me testify," he said.

I smiled. "I can and I will. See you in court, Stanley."

And, sure enough, today is the day that I'm going to see Stanley in court.

**J**udge Hough is not pleased.

I can tell by the way she sneers at me when she takes her seat on the bench. She seems to believe this case is somehow beneath the dignity of her courtroom. I can't imagine she's surprised, though, since I've been lowering the dignity of New Jersey courtrooms, including hers, for more than fifteen years.

Two things have conspired to annoy her even more. For one, she had to hold this hearing on an expedited basis, since there was a thirty-day time limit imposed by the zoning board. It forced her to rejuggle her calendar and postpone matters she thinks are more worthy of her attention.

Secondly, the courtroom is packed with media types and visitors, as the case has semicaptured the attention of the community. This, as she knows all too well, is my fault. I've done a few interviews about it, both on camera and off, and the media has lapped it up with a spoon.

This morning, for example, my friend Vince Sanders, who

is the editor of our local newspaper, ran a picture of an adorable twelve-puppy litter that Pups is caring for in her home. The headline simply said, They learn their fate today, and the subhead said, Will they make it until Christmas?

Stories like that have helped fill the courtroom. There's even a modest overflow crowd outside, many carrying "save the puppies" signs.

It turns out that people like puppies.

Who could have figured that?

Pups is waiting for me when I get to court. She's dressed quite properly in a nice blouse and skirt, as I instructed. She doesn't look particularly comfortable in the outfit; my guess is that she bought it yesterday. I don't think I've ever seen Pups wearing anything other than a Mets sweatshirt or jersey; she and her late husband have always been huge Mets fans.

Also at the table with us is Hike Lynch, the other lawyer at my firm, who works with me on the rare occasions that I take on a client. Hike is a terrific lawyer, but the most pessimistic person I have ever met. I'm sure he thinks this case will end with the puppies being euthanized, tortured, or dropped off a building.

At the table across the way are two city lawyers. I only recognize the lead counsel, Jonathon Witkins, who I'm sure would rather spend the morning being water-boarded. He's a good guy and a talented lawyer but, at barely thirty years old, is still ambitious. I can't imagine he wants to be labeled antipuppy.

Judge Hough has alerted Jonathon and me to the fact that she will not be recessing the trial for lunch, since we had damn well better be done with our cases by then. I don't see why that should be a problem, and I'm sure Jonathon is thinking the shorter, the better.

Because we are the plaintiffs, we present our case first. It's the part I'm most worried about, because our only witness is Pups. She can be a loose cannon; she speaks her mind loudly and frankly, even when she shouldn't. I've tried to coach her for this testimony, but taking coaching does not seem to be Pups's specialty.

Judge Hough tells me to call my first witness, although in this case my first witness is my only one. I call Martha Boyer to the stand, which is likely the first time most people have heard Pups's real name.

Pups stands and half strides, half struts to the witness stand, which is not a good sign. I want her low-key and understated, but her walk doesn't make me confident that she can pull it off.

"Ms. Boyer, do people call you by your given name, or a nickname?"

"They call me Pups."

"Why is that?"

"Because I rescue and take care of puppies."

"How long have you been doing that?"

"Going on twenty-four years."

I take her through a recitation of how she came to do it, where she gets the puppies from, and how she takes care of them. It's a very impressive presentation; Pups does remarkable work.

"How many dogs have you saved, if you know?" I ask.

"Of course I know. You told me to look it up."

The gallery laughs at the fact that she's sassing me, which is OK. It makes her human and more sympathetic. I just hope she doesn't overdo it.

"So I did," I say. "What number did you come up with?"

"Nine thousand seven hundred and sixty-eight."

"How much of your own money have you spent doing this?"

"I don't keep records very well," she says. "Probably sixty thousand a year."

"In twenty-four years, has anyone ever complained about what you're doing?"

"Just once. Three weeks ago."

"How did you find out about it?" I ask.

"I got a notice telling me I needed to stop within thirty days. It said I was breaking the law."

"Did the notice tell you the source of the complaint?" I ask, getting nervous. Here's where Pups might go off the reservation.

"No, they said it was made anonymously."

"OK, then—" I start, but she interrupts me.

"But I know who complained. It was that asshole Hennessey."

This is what I was afraid of. Pups has a new neighbor named Randy Hennessey, and she's sure he's the one who complained. I told her not to mention his name, but she didn't take my advice. If she has to go through this, she at least wants him publicly humiliated.

I ignore the reference and move on. I have her describe the way that she places the dogs in homes once they are old enough. She is very careful and rejects potential adopters if they don't live up to her view of what makes a good dog home, which is often the case.

I end the examination. I only called her to demonstrate her character and commitment and to get on the record what she does for these dogs. That much has been accomplished.

Jonathon must sense the reason for my nervousness, because his first question on cross-examination goes in for the kill. "Ms. Boyer, did you speak to Mr. Hennessey about your suspicion that he made the complaint?"

"You'd better believe it," she says, as I cringe.

"Did he confirm that he did so?"

"No," she says. "The little weasel denied it, but it was obviously a fake denial. My other neighbors told me it was him."

"So you didn't believe him?"

"No way."

"Did you threaten him?"

She thinks for a moment. "Yeah, I guess you could say that."

"I asked you the question. So what did you tell him?"

"That if he caused any more problems, I'd cut his heart out and shove it down his throat."

For some reason, the gallery roars with laughter at this. Jonathon lets her off the stand, probably because he won that round and is afraid of what else she might say.

Pups struts off the stand and takes her seat next to me. It's clear that she thinks she did well, and, all in all, it could have been worse.

Either way, it's OK. Because now it's my turn.

**J**onathon calls Stanley Wade to the stand.

Unlike Pups, who went up there like she was spiking a football, Stanley looks like he's walking the plank. There are even some boos from the gallery, which Judge Hough stifles with a few angry bangs of her gavel.

Jonathon establishes Stanley's job and credentials and then asks him why the zoning board has taken the position that it has in this case.

"The law is clear," Stanley says. "No one in Paterson is allowed to house more than three dogs, unless they have a kennel license."

"Can Ms. Boyer acquire such a license?"

Stanley shakes his head. "No. The area in which she lives does not allow it. A kennel is considered a business, and that area is not zoned for that type of business."

"So you and the board were not making a judgment of any kind . . . you were simply following the law?"

"Yes. That's all we were doing. We don't make the law;

we are charged with enforcing it. It doesn't matter if I like the law or not; I don't have any say in it."

"Thank you. No further questions."

I stand up and walk slowly toward Stanley, who looks like he would hide under the chair if he could. "Mr. Wade, your position, as you've just stated it, is that you are upholding the law, is that correct?"

"Yes."

"Without bias?"

"Correct."

"And you are sworn to uphold the law, no matter whether you agree with it or not? If zoning-law breaking is reported to you, you will step in and act, quickly and decisively?"

"Yes."

"In this case, like all others, you cannot look the other way and allow lawlessness to prevail. You get a complaint, and if it is legitimate, you act. Is that right?"

"Yes."

"Do you like chocolate?" I ask.

He seems surprised and wary, but says, "Sure. Who doesn't?"

I walk over to Hike, who hands me a small bag. "Your Honor, I'd like to introduce these chocolates into evidence."

"I'm sure you'll explain why," the judge says.

I smile. "Imminently." Then I turn to Stanley and say, "These are chocolates made by a company called Candies of Hope. Have you heard of them?"

"Yes."

"They're made by Diane Feller, who happens to be the

wife of Mayor Feller, right here in Paterson. Did you know that?"

"Yes."

"Amazingly, she makes them right in the house where they live. It's all set up in the basement."

Jonathon objects that this is all irrelevant and going nowhere, and Judge Hough tells me to get to the point.

Which I do. "But it turns out that where they live is not zoned for business, and the state of New Jersey defines making and selling chocolates as a business. Isn't that right?"

"She donates the proceeds to charity," Stanley says.

"How nice for her; what a worthy thing to do. Some would say that making chocolate for charity ranks right up there with saving puppies. But the mayor's wife is breaking the law, is she not?"

"Technically."

Hike hands me two pieces of paper, which I submit into evidence. I show the first one to Stanley and ask him if he's ever seen it. He admits that he has, and I ask him to tell the court his understanding of it.

"It's an e-mail complaint about the mayor's wife having a chocolate business in her house."

"Who made the complaint?" I ask.

He reads the name. "Andrea Carper."

"If it please the court," I say, "Andrea Carper is really me, Andy Carpenter. I was deep under cover for this one, so I used my secret identity."

The gallery laughs at this, increasing Stanley's discomfort. Judge Hough gavels them into silence.

I hand Stanley the second piece of paper. "Mr. Wade, is this an e-mail from you responding to Andrea Carper and saying that you would look into the matter?" I ask.

"Yes."

"Did you then threaten the mayor with eviction for breaking the zoning law, in the same manner that you threatened Ms. Boyer?"

"No."

"I'm surprised," I say, "because as a person devoted to the law, I'm sure you share my outrage. Can we assume you will threaten the mayor with eviction when court adjourns? Or would you like to do so right now? I can wait." I take out my cell phone and offer it to him. "You can even use my phone."

He doesn't answer, and Jonathon objects, so I put the phone away and move on.

"Mr. Wade, how did you drive here today?"

"I took Route Four and then city streets," he says.

"While you were on Route Four, did you pass any other cars?"

"I'm sure I did."

"Did you beep your horn as you did so?" I ask.

"No, there was no need to."

"Did you know that there is a New Jersey State law, on the books for the last seventy-one years, that says you have to beep your horn when passing another car? I can quote the statute number if you'd like."

"I didn't know that."

"Ignorance of the law is no excuse. You can turn yourself in to the authorities after you evict the mayor."

Judge Hough says, "Mr. Carpenter, can you move this along?"

I introduce a magazine article into evidence; it's a profile of Judge Hough that ran in the *The Newark Star-Ledger* four years ago. When she looks at it, she says, "Tread carefully, Mr. Carpenter."

I nod. "I will, Your Honor."

I ask Stanley to read a paragraph from the profile that says that the judge lives with her husband, two children, two dogs, and two cats.

"Four pets in one house?" I ask. "Now we have a mayor and a judge about to be put on the street?" By now, the gallery is nearly out of control with laughter.

I don't wait for an answer and instead ask if he knows when the kennel-license law was passed. "No, I don't," he says.

"Eighteen eighty-one," I say. "Are you familiar with the wording?"

"Not entirely."

"Do you know that it refers only to household pets and specifically excludes livestock and farm animals? That area was farmland back then."

"I wasn't aware . . ."

"Is it your position that Ms. Boyer can't care for these puppies, but she can have a houseful of pigs and cows and goats? Is that your position?"

"I—"

I interrupt, though I don't think he even knows how he was going to finish the sentence. "Mr. Wade, Ms. Boyer has been saving puppies in that house for many years. Have you ever had a complaint from a neighbor before?"

"Not that I know of."

"Do you think you can come up with some waivers that prevent the mayor and this fine judge from being homeless and lets poor, abandoned puppies live and find good homes?"

Stanley has been defeated. "Perhaps we can revisit this and . . ."

Judge Hough: "Revisiting this is an excellent idea. I'll hold off on my ruling until you do so. The court will wait to hear the results of your revisitation by the close of business today." She slams down her gavel. "This hearing is adjourned."

I turn to Pups and say, "This one's in the bag."

She's not exactly beaming with relief. "I can't believe that son of a bitch complained."

"Hennessey?"

She nods. "The little twerp."

"Pups, let it go."

She looks at me like I'm out of my mind. "Yeah, right."

**W**e need to talk about our names."

My wife, Laurie Collins, says this after dinner and after our son, Ricky, has gone off to his room. I always enjoy these family dinners, but this one more so than usual, because Laurie spends most of it complimenting my performance in court.

About a half hour ago, I got a call telling me that Stanley's revisiting the issue has resulted in Pups's getting a waiver to continue saving the dogs. I can only hope and pray that the mayor and judge were allowed to stay in their homes as well.

I called Pups to tell her the news, but she wasn't home.

Laurie and I are in the coffee phase of dinner, and she obviously has something she was waiting to talk to me about.

"Our names?" I ask.

She nods. "We need to make some changes."

"You mean like nicknames?" I have no idea what she's talking about.

"No, I mean our last names. Ricky's doing a project at

school, and apparently he had to list our names. He asked me why we all have different names."

Now it makes sense. When Laurie and I married, she wanted to keep her name, Collins, rather than switch to Carpenter. We simultaneously adopted Ricky Diaz, whose father had been murdered not long before that. We never really gave much thought to changing his name at the time; it would have seemed disrespectful to his father.

"So what do you want to do?" I ask.

"At this point, I just want to talk about it."

"OK. You start."

"I think Ricky should have one of our last names, if he wants to," she says.

I nod. "Works for me. Ricky Carpenter has a nice ring to it."

She smiles. "So does Ricky Collins."

I hum, as if it is a lyric, 'Ricky Collins, Ricky Collins." Then I shake my head. "Not really— it has a decent beat, but you can't dance to it. I'd go with Carpenter; it's more modern, more with it."

"Really?" she says, "I've been trying both versions out, and Ricky Carpenter sounds awkward to me. Way too many syllables."

"There's five syllables, and Ricky Collins has four."

She nods. "But that one makes a huge difference. It's twenty-five percent more syllables."

"You could be right," I say, "Let's make it Rick Carpenter. Then we're back to four."

"So you're taking a stand on this?" she says.

"I've got an idea. Why don't we make it Andy, Laurie, and Ricky Carpenter?"

"We've been through this. I like my name."

I nod. "And it's a fine name, an outstanding name. But Carpenter represents New Jersey royalty. You notice Martha took Washington in a heartbeat. Eleanor took Roosevelt. Jackie jumped at Kennedy; you think she thought about staying Jackie Smith?"

"First of all, Jackie Smith was a tight end for the Cowboys," she says. "Jackie Kennedy's maiden name was Bouvier. And when she remarried, she dumped the Kennedy name and took Onassis."

"She would have kept Carpenter."

"I think we should talk to Ricky," she says, effectively ending the conversation. "We can do it when you get home from your walk."

I take Tara, the golden retriever who, in all respects, towers above all other living creatures, and Sebastian, our basset hound, out for their evening walk. It gives me some time to think about the whole name thing with Ricky.

I've never really thought about whether the Carpenter name will live on after me, but if Laurie and I don't have another child, then Ricky is my only shot. I have this feeling that I should care more than I do, but I can't get myself to do so.

We take a fairly brisk walk. It's very cold out, and while Tara has always loved frigid weather, the shorter-haired Sebastian is not a big fan. So he steps up the pace more than usual, probably to get it over with, or maybe to generate warmth.

Many of the houses that we pass have colored Christmas lights all over them, some just tracing the borders of the house, and some with elaborate designs. I've always liked this stuff, and Tara seems OK with it, but Sebastian isn't the festive type. He walks on the other side of the sidewalk whenever we pass a lit-up house.

When I get home, Laurie comes out of the kitchen, talking on the phone. "He just walked in, Willie," she says, walking toward me with the phone.

Willie Miller is my former client, current friend, and partner in the Tara Foundation, a rescue operation that we run. The foundation is named after my aforementioned wonderful golden retriever. "Can you tell him I'll call him right back?" I ask, wanting to get out of my coat and get the dogs' leashes off them.

She shakes her head and hands me the phone. "I don't think that's a good idea."

It's a strange thing for her to say, but the only way I'm going to find out what's going on is to take the phone. "Willie?" I say, moving the conversation right along.

"I'm at Pups'," he says. I knew that he was going there to drop off two puppies we had at the foundation. We were just waiting to get her case resolved before doing so. "You'd better get down here."

"What's wrong?"

"The police are here. They've got her under arrest."

This is not computing. "Why?"

"Well, I only got to talk to her for a second. But it sounds like they think she murdered someone."

"Is that what she said?"

"No, I overheard it from one of the cops. Pete was here also, but he didn't see me, and he left."

"Who was murdered?"

"I don't know," he says.

"What did Pups say when you talked to her?" I ask.

"She said, 'call Andy.'"

I give the phone back to Laurie and zip my coat back up.

"Call me and let me know what's going on," she says. Laurie likes Pups . . . always has.

"I will. And if you talk to Ricky, tell him I vote for Carpenter."

**P**ete, it's me, Andy," I say into my cell phone. "I knew that," he says. "My caller ID said, 'slimeball defense attorney.'"

Pete Stanton is actually one of my best friends in the world, but as a captain in the homicide division of the Paterson police, he seems not to have a great respect for my profession.

I ignore the insult. "What the hell is going on with Pups?"

"What do I look like, CNN?" he asks.

"Do I have to play my attorney-client chip?" I successfully defended Pete a few years ago when he himself was wrongly accused of murder. Not only did I get him off, but I didn't charge him for the defense. In the world of guilt infliction, that ranks as a weapon of mass destruction.

The truth is that I know he's incredibly grateful to me, even though it would break the code for him to admit it. But he's not grateful enough to help a person he considers a murderer get off, so he's still going to give me a hard time.

"The guy she killed was one Randall Hennessey; they apparently had a dispute over some dogs, and she figured that shooting him in the head would swing the argument in her favor."

"Any witnesses?"

"A neighbor saw her running out of his house."

"Murder weapon?" I ask.

"Is this particular murderer your client?"

Pete apparently is unaware of the courtroom hearing this afternoon. I'm not surprised; other than his work, the only thing he cares about is sports.

"If you are talking about the alleged murderer, she is," I say. "Where is she?"

"She's at County being processed; the alleged dead body is at the coroner, where it will be determined whether the bullet that blew open the top of his head had anything to do with the cause of death."

"I need a favor," I say.

He laughs. "You want to plead it down to jaywalking?"

"No. There are a bunch of dogs in her house. I want you to get word to your people that Willie and I can go in and get them."

"What the hell is it with you and dogs?" he says. "Besides, it's not my case. I was just there in a supervisory capacity, because I'm a big shot. It's Luther Crenshaw's case."

"I don't care if it's J. Edgar Hoover's case; you can get this done. Now will you just take care of it?"

"It's an active scene," he says. "Our people are searching it."

"We'll just go in and get them, and your people can watch us the whole time. Come on, even you can't want puppies to starve to death."

He's quiet for at least fifteen seconds, apparently weighing the starving puppies versus the favor-to-the-defense-lawyer conundrum. Finally, "OK. ten minutes. I'll make the call."

"You're a real softie."

I head to Pup's house, which is pretty close by. I don't bother calling Willie; I know he won't have left. He'll be thinking about the dogs as well.

Sure enough, he's standing just outside the police barricades. He obviously called his wife, Sondra, who is there with him. She works full-time with him at the Tara Foundation.

"They won't let us get the dogs," he says.

I nod and walk over to a cop that I know, a sergeant named Alan Silver. He's never been a fan of mine, especially since I once made him look bad in a cross-examination.

"Captain Stanton call you?" I ask.

"Yeah, he called. You got ten minutes." He looks at his watch. "Now it's nine minutes and fifty-five seconds."

I signal for Willie and Sondra to join me. We get all the dogs out of the house with two minutes to spare. We have no need to take any of the equipment, because we have all of it at the foundation. Willie grabs a bag of food, because we have mostly adult dog food, and this is specially made for puppies.

Sondra has brought the van that we use to pick up dogs from the shelter, so we load them all in there. There are twelve puppies, the mother, and Pups's own pet, an adorable miniature toy poodle named Puddles. "You guys going to be OK from here?" I ask. "I need to get down to the jail."

"We're fine," Sondra says.

"Everything's cool," Willie says, echoing her sentiment. "Did Pups kill that guy?"

"I don't know," I say. "What do you think?"

"Damn," he says. "There've been times I thought she was going to kill me."

I head down to the county jail and tell the guy at the reception desk that I'm Martha Boyer's attorney and that I want to see her. He must be new, because I've never seen him before, and I've spent plenty of time down here.

"You're a little late," he says.

"What does that mean?"

"They just wheeled her out of here. I think she had a heart attack."

I head for St. Joseph's Hospital.

It's the only full-service hospital in Paterson since the Barnert Hospital closed, so it's a pretty good bet that St. Joe's is where they took Pups. I was born at St. Joe's, yet when I pull up I notice that they still have not erected a statue commemorating that fact.

There are two police cars in front of the emergency room, which is not exactly a shocking event here in downtown Paterson. I park and go in, and again see Sergeant Silver, who has obviously just been redeployed here. It's a break for me, because the phone call from Pete has given me some credibility when it comes to access.

He half sneers when he sees me. "So everyone is right," he says. "You really are an ambulance chaser."

"Don't ever lose that wit," I say. "What's going on with my client?"

"She collapsed at the jail, and they took her here. Might be bullshit. We're waiting to find out."

My heart warmed by his compassion, I head upstairs to

the cardiology department. Once there, I go to the nurses' station and introduce myself as Pups's attorney. "How and where is she?" I ask.

"She's in the intensive care unit, being examined and treated by Dr. Sonaya."

"Will Dr. Sonaya come out here when he's finished?"

"She just did," a voice says, emphasizing the "she." I look over and see a doctor who is definitely female walking up to me. "What can I do for you?"

"I'm Martha Boyer's attorney. How is she?"

She hesitates, as if choosing her words. "How much about Ms. Boyer's health issues do you know?"

It seems a somewhat strange question to ask. "Just that she collapsed and was brought here."

She nods. "Give me a few minutes." Then she goes back in the direction that she came from.

A few minutes becomes ten, and as I'm starting to wonder if she'll ever come back, she does. "I just needed to get clearance from Ms. Boyer," she says. "Confidentiality."

"Did she have a heart attack?" I ask.

She shakes her head. "No. She suffered what is called supraventricular tachycardia, which is basically a dramatic increase in heart rate. It can be brought on by stress or intense emotion. Based on the police involvement, my guess is she's had plenty of both today."

"That's for sure. Is she going to be OK?"

Another hesitation. "This time I believe she will. We'll monitor her closely for a couple of days, but if there are no further complications, I would be optimistic that she will recover from this event. But it's a serious condition, and she'll need to be on medication."

"Can I talk to her?"

"No, not now, but she knows that you are here. Is there a message you want conveyed to her?"

"Just please tell her not to talk about her case to anyone but me."

She nods. "I can do that."

She tells me that Pups should be able to see me tomorrow or the next day at the latest. Since there's no reason for me to hang around anymore, I head back home.

Local news radio is already all over the story, and, as always, the unspoken initial assumption is that the police are probably right and that Pups is probably guilty.

It's been quite a day for Pups, going from a courtroom victory to a charge of murder to a semi–heart attack. I'm both looking forward to and dreading hearing her side of the story. Pups is not necessarily the most stable person in the world, and I know how angry she was at Hennessey. Even worse, she announced in court how she threatened to "cut his heart out and shove it down his throat." If the autopsy shows his heart stuck in his throat, that could be a problem.

I can't really even think about how I might defend her until I know all the circumstances and have heard her side of the story. So for now I'll just hope that she has a cousin whom she considers the best defense attorney on the planet, and who is chomping at the bit to take on her case.

It's almost midnight when I get home, and I'm exhausted. Laurie has waited up for me and, naturally, wants to be updated on the night's events. Her being an ex-cop, I know that Laurie's initial inclination is to side with the police, but she just listens and doesn't openly take a side.

"What effect will her being in the hospital have on the process?" she asks.

"She won't be arraigned until she's physically capable of it. My sense is that it won't be more than a few days; being arraigned is not exactly physically taxing. When she's able to be up and about, they'll get her into court."

"You ready for bed?" she asks.

That is not a tough call, since the last time I wasn't ready for bed with Laurie was never.

**A**t this point, there is no sense getting our investigative team together.

We don't know anything, and we won't be receiving any discovery information until Pups is arraigned. The media is painting it as a simple story; the police believe that Pups got revenge on Hennessey for trying to get her evicted and shot him.

I head down to the hospital and am pleased to learn that she is doing very well and is in the process of being taken out of intensive care. I send in word that I'm there and want to see her, and the response that comes back is positive.

I am going to have to wait for at least an hour, so I head for the lounge. The place is filled with Christmas decorations in a completely unsuccessful attempt to make it look something other than depressing.

There are two police officers present, no doubt to prevent Pups from breaking out of intensive care and making a run for it. I assume that they know me, because they give me the typical sneer; they must learn sneering at the police academy. I smile sweetly in return.

I get some coffee out of the vending machine. After one taste, I fight the urge to spit it out; it tastes like it has come directly out of the Passaic River. It's so awful that I offer to buy the officers some. They accept, so I'm able to get a little bit of liquid revenge for the sneering.

When I'm finally led into Pups's room, I'm taken aback by what I see. She's still hooked up to a bunch of tubes and wires, and she looks ten years older than the last time I saw her, which was less than twenty-four hours ago. There is something else about her that I have never seen before.

She looks vulnerable.

And scared.

"Where are the dogs?" is the first thing she asks.

"Willie has them. They're fine."

"You get Puddles also?"

Pups is totally devoted to her toy poodle. "Of course," I say. "Willie says she has already laid claim to the couch."

She smiles. "Good." Then, "You gonna help me deal with this crap?"

"That's why I'm here."

"I didn't kill the son of a bitch. I would have, without losing a wink of sleep, but I didn't. It's all a bunch of garbage."

"Do you know who did?"

"No."

"You up to telling me what happened?"

She nods, but starts to cough before she speaks. It's a fairly violent cough; I'm afraid she's going to disconnect the tubes. Finally, she says, "He called me."

"Hennessey?"

She frowns. "No, Gandhi. Of course it was Hennessey. He called me and told me he wanted to talk to me, that he wanted to apologize."

"What did you say?"

"That he should kiss my ass."

I nod. "Nice and conciliatory. What happened then?"

"He asked me to come over; said he wanted to talk and give me something, a gift for the dogs. He said he felt terrible about the whole thing and wanted to be a good neighbor."

"So you went?"

She nods. "I went. When I got there, I rang the bell, and he yelled out that the door was open and I should come in. He said he was in the kitchen. So I went in, and I didn't see him there, so I opened a door that I figured might be the kitchen."

"Was it the kitchen?" I ask.

"Yes, and he was in there. He was lying on the floor with half his head blown off."

"What did you do?"

"I got the hell out of there and went home. And then I called 911 and told them what was going on. When I heard the sirens a couple of minutes later, I went out to meet them. But they told me to wait outside; they wouldn't let me back in his house. Which was OK with me; I didn't want to have to see that again."

"What happened next?"

"They told me to wait in the police car, that they would need to question me. I was stuck in there for two hours, and when they finally came over, they read me my rights and arrested me."

"I'm confused about something," I say. "If he was dead on the floor of the kitchen, how did he call out to you to come in?"

"Good question, Sherlock."

"Did you know his voice well enough to recognize it?"

She shakes her head. "No."

"Did the voice on the phone sound like the voice in the house?"

She shrugs. "I don't know. Maybe."

"Did you hear any other noises, like someone else might have been in the house?"

"No."

"Do you own a gun?"

"Who am I? Annie Oakley? No; they scare the hell out of me."

Pups can be a tad caustic, and the events of the last twenty-four hours seem to have darkened her mood somewhat. But I press on. "And you have no idea why the police think you did it?"

"The only thing I can think of is that I talked about him in court and sort of threatened him."

I don't want to say it to her now, but they must have more than that if they placed her under arrest.

"OK," I say. "We'll find out what they have and go from there. How are you feeling?"

"Better than yesterday, worse than every other day of my life."

"OK, get some rest and I'll tell you when I learn more."

"So you're my lawyer?"

"If you want me," I say.

"You're probably no worse than anybody else I'd get."

"Stop it," I say. "You're making me blush."

**J** ason Ridgeway did not see how things could be going better.

It'd been some year for Ridgeway, actually some two years. An obscure town councilman, he had agreed to run for state senate. The offer had been made to him because it was not exactly a coveted slot; everyone with any knowledge of South Dakota politics considered it a quixotic effort. It was a district solidly in the opposition party's corner and occupied by a popular incumbent.

Two weeks before the election, that popular incumbent had become decidedly less popular, when it was revealed that he had been accepting bribes for as many years as he had been in office.

It was too late for his party to remove him from the ballot, and since very few people were willing to vote for a known thief, Ridgeway became the default winner.

Young and good-looking, he had latched on to a few popular local initiatives and was making a name for himself. The party saw in him a potential national candidate, which is why they gave him significant committee assignments, the most recent being the chairman of the Environment and Natural Resources Committee. In South Dakota, they take their environment and natural resources pretty seriously.

With the job came some perks—not national-level perks; South Dakota state senators don't get to ride on Air Force One—and this weekend was an example of those perks: Ridgeway was attending a three-day EPA meeting of local environmental leaders, inside and outside the government, held in Las Vegas.

Ridgeway had never been to Vegas before. Until this weekend, he'd considered Omaha "the big city." Except for the meetings themselves, which were quite boring, he'd loved every minute of the trip.

Especially last night.

The delegates, Ridgeway included, were staying on the strip at the Mirage. Last night, while most of his colleagues were in the casino, Ridgeway took a cab downtown. He wasn't much of a gambler, anyway, and didn't have much money to waste.

He found a really great hotel bar and had a drink. One drink became five, maybe six, and the next thing he knew there was a great-looking woman next to him, hanging on his every slurred word.

If Ridgeway was honest with himself, he wouldn't blame the alcohol. Once she put her hand on the inside of his leg, he didn't have a chance. He would have followed her anywhere, even if he had been drinking club soda.

At least he was smart enough not to bring her back to his hotel. She was already staying at this particular hotel, so they just went upstairs to her room. He didn't have to check in, and, as far as he could remember, he never even told her his name.

Nothing could be traced back to him; it was as if it never happened. And the truth is that he didn't really regret what he did; it was fantastic, and an experience that he knew would truly be once in a lifetime. And it had to be; with his wife and two kids at home, any revelation of this type of behavior would destroy both his political career and his personal life.

So he would never do it again, but he sure had the memory of this one time. Having breakfast at the Mirage and planning to head to the airport in a couple of hours, it was really all he could think about.

He was sitting alone and just about finished when a man came over to the table. "Senator Ridgeway?" the man asked, a smile on his face.

"That's me."

"I just wanted to say hello. My name is Caffey. I'm a big fan, and I know you're going places. I want to be able to tell people I knew you when."

Ridgeway laughed. "Well, you can tell them that."

The man smiled again. "I think I'll just do that." He turned to walk away but then stopped and said, "Hey, I hope you don't mind, but can I take a selfie with you? People back home will get a kick out of it."

"Sure. Why not?"

The man took out a cell phone and moved next to Ridgeway, leaning over so that their heads were next to each other. He held up the phone, and Ridgeway looked toward it. But he didn't see the image of himself and the stranger.

He saw the woman from last night, in her room.

With an icon that indicated it was a video.

"Press play when you get to your room and no one is around, Senator. You can keep the phone; I've got other copies."

Ridgeway tried to say something, but, in his horror, words did not come out.

"One vote, Senator. We're going to call on you for one vote, and then we'll be out of your life. It won't hurt a bit."

And then he walked away.

**G**etting ready for a fun holiday?"

The voice is Rita Gordon, the clerk at the Passaic County courthouse. Rita knows me very well, and she knows that preparing to try a murder case is not my idea of a joyous holiday season.

Rita even knows me in the biblical sense, though I'm not sure the forty-five-minute affair we once had would even register on the official list of biblical dos and don'ts. It was during a brief period when Laurie had left me and moved to her home town in Wisconsin, and I haven't mentioned it to Rita since because it seems awkward to do so. Rita hasn't mentioned it either, and I'm afraid that it's because she's forgotten it even happened.

"Totally," I say. "I'm already covered in tinsel."

"Sounds adorable, but tomorrow is suit-and-tie day."

"The arraignment? My client is still in the hospital."

"Not as of four o'clock today. She's getting out, and the justice system is chomping at the bit to have a shot at her."

"Who's got the case?"

49

"Judge Harrison Chambers."

"Shit." Judge Harrison Chambers is a hard-ass, old-time jurist. I think he decided to be a judge at the age of zero, probably because of his name. It's like the old Seinfeld joke about the fact that naming a child Jeeves pretty much ensures that he's going to be a butler rather than an auto mechanic.

There's never a shortage of dirty jokes about what happens when Judge Harrison Chambers invites you back to his chambers.

"Your bad luck," she says, "He's retiring in six months. You should have told your client to wait before she killed the guy."

There's no sense in telling Rita about the alleged nature of the charge or the whole "innocent until proved guilty" thing; she's only kidding with me. "Who's the prosecutor?" I ask.

"Dan Tressel."

"The new kid?" Tressel is maybe thirty-three and new to the prosecutor's office. He's rumored to be ambitious, which is no great sin, unless he tries to make the climb by stepping on defense attorneys.

Rita laughs. "Yeah, he's stopping by briefly on the way to the governor's mansion."

I get off the phone with Rita and place a call to Dan Tressel, who keeps me waiting for five minutes before coming to the phone. Finally, "Tressel here."

"Andy Carpenter here," is me, responding in kind.

"What is this in reference to?" he says.

He's pretending he doesn't know me or why I am calling. It's an attempt for him to show superiority, and to get me feeling humiliated and angry. He thinks it will establish a relationship between us that will help him at trial.

If he thinks he'll get me angry and looking for revenge, he doesn't know Andy Carpenter. I will remain calm and unruffled as I rip his stinking heart out and feed it to the jury. "I'm calling about getting discovery material on the Martha Boyer case."

"Oh, right," he says, as if he's handed a murder trial every day, and this one slipped his mind. Then, "The arraignment is tomorrow."

Prosecutors legally don't have to start handing over discovery material until two things happen. One is the defense attorney's requesting it, a formality I'm attempting to go through now. The other is for the arraignment to be concluded. "I thought I'd give us a head start."

"Good thought, but let's stick to the rules," he says.

"Wow, you're really intimidating," I say. "It's going to take all my courage just to show up tomorrow."

"See you at the arraignment," he says, and hangs up.

I hang up as well, having accomplished absolutely nothing. So if I'm going to spend my time doing nothing productive, I might as well do it with a beer in my hand.

I head to Charlie's, the sports bar that I used to go to almost every night. Since Laurie and I married and adopted Ricky, I've become a family man and reduced my Charlie's attendance to two or three times a week. You can't say I haven't matured.

Speaking of people who haven't matured, Pete Stanton and Vince Sanders are already at our regular table when I arrive.

It's a big night; the Giants are playing the Eagles on Thursday-night football, and every one of the thirty televisions has the pregame show on.

Vince is the editor of the local newspaper, and I would think he could get credentials to go to the game as a reporter, but he'd never consider it. This restaurant, at this table, is where he always wants to be. I'm sure that it must say in his will that when he dies, his ashes are to be spread throughout Charlie's. I probably won't be ordering any food here that week.

Pete would also never miss a football game at Charlie's. If I were going to commit a murder in Paterson, I'd do it during a game, because the ranking homicide captain wouldn't show up on the scene until the game was decided.

"Where have you been?" Vince asks. "The game's about to start. We held up on ordering because we thought we might have to pay the check."

"God forbid."

Vince calls out to the waitress. "He's here," he says. "Start bringing the beer and burgers."

Pete has nothing to say; he's too focused on the opening kickoff. I'm a football nut, but Pete makes me look normal. He won't open his mouth until halftime, except to ingest beer and food, and occasionally yell profanities at the refs and "Make a play!" at the Giants. He thinks it would never enter their mind to make a play unless he screamed it to them from Charlie's.

The Giants are up by two touchdowns at the half, so we're all in a pretty good mood and will remain so until and unless the Giants start blowing it in the third quarter.

"So did you find the real killer yet, counselor?" Pete asks.

"Maybe a Colombian drug gang?" It's a decades-old reference to an attempt O. J. Simpson's lawyers made to point to someone other than their client.

"That process starts tomorrow," I say. "And, once again, it will culminate in my total destruction of you on the witness stand."

He laughs, knowing as I do that our previous witness-stand battles have been fairly even matches. "Not me; Luther Crenshaw is your man, and he'll eat you alive. Is your client healthy enough to go on trial? Or is her plan to die before the jury starts deliberating?"

"You wouldn't want to get in the ring with her," I say. "Besides, I'll get the damn thing dismissed before it sees the inside of a courtroom."

He laughs again, this time even harder. "You obviously haven't started getting discovery yet."

"No, Tressel is holding out until the arraignment."

"I can't stand that little shithead," Pete says. "He almost makes me root for you."

"They have a murder weapon?" I ask.

He nods. "Freshly fired and recovered from your client's basement. And that's not the worst part. Or, from my point of view, the best part."

That's pretty bad; if there's something worse than that, I can't imagine right now what it would be. "What's the worst part?" I ask.

"You'll find out."

"Come on, I'll get the discovery tomorrow," I say. "How can it hurt to tell me now?"

He thinks for a moment. "If you tell anyone it came from me, I'll strangle you."

"Fair enough."

"You remember when her husband and that gangbanger got gunned down in front of that restaurant? Like eighteen months ago?"

"Of course."

He smiles, relishing the moment.

"Same gun," he says.

**T**he news is so stunning that I do something unprecedented . . . I leave Charlie's before the Giants game is over.

I stay until mid–third quarter, but the need to get home and do some research is too great. By the time the fourth quarter starts, with the Giants now ahead by three touchdowns, I'm by my computer.

I go online to check out the details of the shooting in which Jake Boyer died a year and a half ago. Laurie remembers it better than I do, and the newspaper stories confirm her recollections.

Jake Boyer was having dinner with a man named David Barnett, identified in the stories as a business associate. It doesn't say what the business was, and I actually have no idea what Jake Boyer did for a living. They were leaving the restaurant and had reached their car when a vehicle drove up and fired five shots. Two of them hit and killed Boyer, and a third hit and killed Raymond "Little Tiny" Parker, a local gang member. The fourth and fifth bullets hit a Chevrolet

Malibu, which apparently was treated at the scene and re-leased.

Both the police and the writer of every article I am able to find believed that the target was Parker, misnamed Little Tiny because he was six foot four, 250 pounds. Everyone felt that Boyer and Barnett were unfortunate bystanders, Boyer being by far the more unfortunate of the two.

Despite pleas for people to call in with information, the cops came up empty. There were follow-up stories, decreas-ing in frequency, for a couple of months, but the story pe-tered out from lack of new information. I'm quite sure the case was never solved, because if it was, then there would have been a media reaction.

I've never really talked to Pups about it, though I did at-tend the funeral and, of course, express my condolences. I don't think that there was the slightest hint, then or since, that she might have done the shooting or that Jake was the actual target.

But if the same gun that killed Jake Boyer and Little Tiny Parker also killed Hennessey, and if that gun was found in Pups's basement, then there is no doubt she is in the police crosshairs for all the killings.

I still know very little about this case, but I know it just got a hell of a lot harder.

I don't have a great night's sleep, and I actually watch the last half of the Giants game on DVR at three in the morn-ing. I do it with the sound off, since Laurie doesn't seem to be sharing my insomnia. It ends with one of those rare events, a Giants wire-to-wire win.

The arraignment is at ten AM, but I've arranged to have Pups brought there an hour early so that we can discuss what is going to take place in court. I don't think she's ever been arrested or arraigned before, but there just may be a lot I don't know about Pups. For all I know, she could have been tried for war crimes at The Hague.

When she's brought into the anteroom, she's in a wheelchair, and her wrists are handcuffed to the arms of the chair. Nevertheless, she looks better than the last time I saw her; her face has considerably more color to it. And I can tell by the look in her eyes that her feistiness is back.

I'm not going to talk to her about the gun or about her dead husband. Part of the reason is my promise to Pete that I wouldn't say anything, but it's more that this just isn't the time or place. When I get the discovery and can read the details, I'll have a long conversation with Pups about the case and about the gun.

So for now I confine our conversation to the arraignment itself. Very little will happen of great significance; the charges will be presented, and she will have a chance to plead. If she pleads not guilty, a trial date will probably be set.

After I set the ground rules, I ask, "Have you thought about what you would like your plea to be?"

"Are you kidding? Not guilty."

"OK; when they ask you, just say it firmly. And just those two words; don't editorialize. You're going to hate the prosecutor, but no mouthing off at him. That's exactly what he would want you to do."

"Got it."

"Good. Now for the ground rules. If I'm going to be your lawyer, then I'm in charge. You do exactly what I say; we can discuss things, but ultimately I will call the shots."

She looks hesitant, so I say, "The alternative is to find another lawyer who will let you make decisions, and if that's what you want, then I can recommend some people."

"OK," she says, but with obvious reluctance. "You're in charge. Except for one thing; you have to give me one thing."

"What's that?"

"A fast trial. As soon as possible."

"That is not in your best interest," I say.

She nods. "I believe you. But I have to have it. If you can't give that to me, then I really do need to find another lawyer. But it's you I want."

I nod. "OK. I can live with that."

"Thank you," she says. "Is there anything else you wanted to tell me?"

"One more thing. You tell me the truth. Always. Every time. If you don't, it will bite you in the ass."

"I always tell the truth, to you and everybody else."

I believe that; I've always known it about her. So I let it drop, and we head in for the hearing.

"Showtime," I say.

Judge Chambers's reputation is well deserved.

He's known as a no-nonsense judge who moves things along, one who won't tolerate a wasted moment. I don't have very much direct experience with him, but he certainly runs the arraignment in that manner.

The charges are read, and I'm not surprised that there is no mention of the possibility of adding a charge for the second and third murders, that of Jake Boyer and Little Tiny Parker. Tressel would probably want to hold those in reserve on the off chance that if he loses this trial, the other charges would give him additional bites at the apple.

Pups is called on to enter a plea, and she doesn't disappoint. She clearly and with determination says, "Not guilty, Your Honor."

I request bail, though it's just a formality. There is no chance that the request will be granted, and Judge Chambers dispenses with it quickly. He then asks the attorneys if there are any other issues to discuss.

Tressel stands. "One more, Your Honor. But it's of a sensitive nature, so I would request that we discuss it privately, in closed session in chambers."

I'm taken by surprise, and Chambers seems to be as well. My guess is that it has something to do with the other murders, but I don't know why that would be relevant to these proceedings or why it couldn't be discussed in open court. Maybe Tressel wants to have his cake and eat it too, by not charging Pups for the other murders but being allowed to introduce them as evidence at trial.

Once we're back in chambers, the judge says to Tressel, "Let's hear it."

"Judge, there are special circumstances relating to the timing of the trial, and I would like to get our position on record, and learn Your Honor's feelings about it. I assume the defense is planning to weigh in as well."

I have no idea what he's talking about but don't want to say so, so I let Judge Chambers carry the ball.

"What are you talking about?" he asks.

"The defendant's medical condition."

"I thought that since she had already recovered sufficiently to attend this hearing, that she would be well enough to stand trial," Chambers says. "Do you have other information that I am not aware of?"

Tressel looks over at me quickly to see if I'm going to jump in, but I'm not. "In the course of reviewing information from the hospital regarding her ability to be here today, we took note of other information that was part of the examination. Her medical history."

"And?" the judge asks, showing some impatience.

"The defendant suffers from malignant mesothelioma. It is a terminal condition and has already resisted the conventional treatments. I am told that while there can be some symptom relief, the outcome is assured, and she has been given a prognosis of six months to a year to live."

I try not to reveal my shock, but I would have considered it just as likely that Tressel would have said that aliens descended on the earth and murdered Hennessey.

Judge Chambers turns to me. "Mr. Carpenter, would you like to address this matter?"

There's no sense lying. "I certainly would, Your Honor, but I'm going to need a little time. This is the first I have heard of this."

He nods. "Very well. Then there is no sense in my making a ruling. But if the seriousness of the illness can be independently confirmed, then I can tell you I may look negatively at using the state's resources to try and convict a person who may not live long enough to be sentenced."

Tressel doesn't like hearing this. "Your Honor, medical prognoses can be wrong, sometimes dramatically so. But even if this one is correct, the state of New Jersey has an interest in criminals being brought to justice, regardless of what their future holds."

"I imagine the defense might have a different view," the judge says, and then looks straight at me. "It is a view I expect to hear shortly."

I nod. "You will, Your Honor."

We head back into court. I'm still stunned by what I've

just heard. To the extent I've thought about it at all, I've always assumed Pups's cough was insignificant, maybe even a nervous habit. I never imagined it was a symptom of a life-ending disease.

When I reach the defense table, Pups leans over to me and whispers, "What was that about?"

"I'll tell you after court."

Judge Chambers wraps things up by announcing that there will be a delay in setting a trial date, with the agreement of both the prosecution and defense. I can see that Pups is not happy, and now I know why she wants to rush this process. She has very little time left to enjoy life, even if she wins.

I arrange with the bailiff for an additional ten minutes with Pups back in the anteroom after the judge adjourns the hearing. He wheels her in there, and when he leaves, I turn to her and say, "You're going to die?"

She smiles and says, "We all are, honey. We all are."

I'm not sure what question to ask first.

The one that comes to mind is, Why the hell didn't you tell me? but that seems a bit insensitive. Pups is dying, and I'm not sure I should make this about me.

So I just start with, "Tell me about it."

"I have a cancer called mesothelioma; people get it from being exposed to asbestos. Not like yesterday or last month; the thing takes decades to come out. My father had a small factory that manufactured construction materials. Nobody thought about it then, but it must have been asbestos city."

"How long have you known about it?" I ask.

"Almost two years, a little less. I was going through all kinds of treatments, but nothing worked. All it did was prolong the inevitable."

"And you've been to the best doctors?"

"Oh, I should be going to doctors? I've been letting a nurse practitioner handle the whole thing." She shakes her head at the idiocy of my question. "Of course I've been to the best doctors. You think I want to die? I went to Sloan Kettering. Once they saw normal treatments weren't working, they tried some experimental stuff. Nothing took. Now I'm basically just dealing with the symptoms."

I nod. "OK, well I'm sure you know how sorry I am about this. But for now, we need to talk about it as it relates to this case."

"It has nothing to do with this case," she says.

"Yes, it does. You most likely don't have to go through a trial at all; the judge would delay it long enough for . . . for it not to matter."

"But I'd sit in jail for the rest of my life?"

"Yes," I say. "There's no way around that."

"And people would always assume I was a murderer?"

"Probably."

"Wow . . . that sounds like a terrific deal. We should grab it. Did you win your law degree in a raffle?"

I can't stifle a laugh; she has nailed the situation pretty well. But I try a different tack. "A trial is not going to be a pleasant experience."

"Unless we win."

"Even then," I say.

"Better than sitting in a cell, waiting to die. I did not do this, and I'm not going to let anyone believe that I did."

I'm not going to talk her out of this, and, as much as I dread preparing for a murder trial, I'm not sure I want to. I'm not big on screwing around with dying wishes.

I nod. "OK, we go to trial. We don't have time to talk now,

so I'll set up a meeting to go over things. But in the meantime, there's something I want you to think about."

"Good. I have plenty of time."

"The gun that killed Hennessey was found in your basement."

"That's a bunch of crap," she says.

I shake my head. "No, it's true. And there's more."

"Let's hear it."

"It's the same gun that killed your husband."

I can tell that she is stunned by this. Of course, that doesn't necessarily mean she's innocent. It could mean that she is surprised the police discovered the connection.

"That can't be," she says.

"I'm told that the forensics are conclusive," I say. "But I'll be getting more details."

She's trying to formulate her thoughts, but it's not easy to do. "I don't even know where to go with this. What does it mean?"

"I'm not even close to answering that question," I say. "But for now I want you to think about a couple of things. One, although at the time everyone thought Jake was in the wrong place at the wrong time that night, it's possible he was the target. Try and think of why that could be and who might have wanted him dead."

"Wanted Jake dead?" she asks, as if she is rolling the idea around in her mind.

"And think if there's any connection between Hennessey and Jake."

"There can't be," she says. "Hennessey moved in long after Jake died."

"That's the wrong way to approach it. Assume there's a connection, and try to figure out what it is."

She nods her agreement, but I can see that she just doesn't fully accept what I'm telling her. "What are you going to do?" she asks.

"I'm going to try and let you die with dignity."

If there is anything more boring than arraignment number 1, it's arraignment number 2.

Not that this is a full arraignment; the only purpose is to decide whether to set a trial date. Judge Chambers wants to do it in the courtroom with a court reporter, but, in deference to the confidential medical information that could be discussed, he does not allow spectators or media to attend. Since I know what is going to happen, I don't even bother to tell Hike to show up. I can handle this on my own.

Once the judge is seated, he asks me what is the defense's position on holding or delaying a trial. "We absolutely want a trial, Your Honor, and we invoke our right to a speedy one."

I detect a slight frown on the judge's face, but he simply turns to the prosecution. "Mr. Tressel?"

Tressel stands up. "The prosecution can be ready very quickly, Your Honor."

Chambers nods. "Very well. I am hereby ordering a medical examination, the purpose of which is to assure the court that Ms. Boyer will be physically able to stand trial. If that answer comes back in the positive, I will provide you both with a date at the earliest possible time."

He adjourns the hearing, and I tell Pups that I will see her soon, probably tomorrow.

"Give 'em hell," she says. "And give it to 'em fast."

I nod. "Fast hell, that's what I'll give them. As soon as I figure out how."

I tend to think of myself as an unconventional attorney; I sort of wear it as a badge of honor. But the truth is that I am a creature of habit. I approach each case in the same manner. I try and look at the big picture, and I do everything I can not to let my predeterminations and biases lead me in a particular direction.

I also always take two initial steps, regardless of the case. The first is to visit the scene of the crime, when that is at all possible. I don't necessarily learn that much, but it somehow clears my head and brings me emotionally into the case. The second thing I always do is convene a meeting of our investigative and legal team.

My first call is to Laurie, to tell her that I'll pick her up and take her to the crime scene. As a former police detective and my chief investigator, she can assess it with a more practiced eye than I can.

I then call Pete Stanton, to arrange for us to be allowed into the scene. He once again tells me that it's Luther Crenshaw's case, but he agrees to do so anyway, since he knows I can gain admittance through the court if he or Luther resisted. "I'm sure you'll crack the case," he says, rather drily.

"When I find the real killer, I'll bring him in to you," I say. "Try not to screw up reading him his Miranda rights. Sound out the words phonetically."

My third call is to Hike, to tell him to officially request discovery and to round up the team for an early afternoon meeting. "She's not pleading it out?" he asks, in obvious surprise and disappointment.

"No, we're going to trial."

"But she's got three months to live," he says.

"Actually, she's been told six to twelve months."

"They always guess long," he says. "She'll be history in three, four months tops. Vegas will be taking bets on whether she makes it through jury selection."

"Stay upbeat, Hike."

Laurie meets me in front of the house when I pull up. It's just a short ride to the scene, but she has time to inform me that the media has broken the story of Pups's illness.

I'm embarrassed for Pups; it can't be pleasant to have her intimate health details out there for the world to see. In terms of the case, it probably cuts in our favor. The public, including the future jurors, would possibly see this as a heroic fight to prove her innocence and save her reputation before dying. What other reason could she have for going down this road?

There is one police officer on the porch of Hennessey's house when we arrive. There's also police tape surrounding the entrances to the house, and I'm not sure if the cop is assigned here or if he's here because Pete knew we were coming. Either way, Laurie knows him from her days on the force, so he lets us right in.

Hennessey was new to the area, having moved in only three months before his death. He doesn't seem to have been a type A personality, since there are a number of boxes that he hadn't gotten around to unpacking.

I'm the same way; if I were living alone and moved to someplace new, I'd probably never unpack. Laurie, on the other hand, would have the place looking like she lived there for ten years before the moving men left.

The den area looks fairly undisturbed, except for the residue that shows that fingerprints were lifted throughout. We go into the kitchen, and it's not too hard to tell where Hennessey was shot; the blood and chalk marks are still on the floor.

It's always weird to be in a place where someone has recently died a violent death. The incident has long since happened, but you can almost feel the violence and fear in the air.

"My guess is we'll find out that Hennessey was shot in the back," Laurie says.

"Why do you say that?"

"Because it happened here, near the door. It seems unlikely that he was surprised to find someone hiding in the kitchen; it's more likely that he was talking with his killer, and then tried to get out when he realized what was about to happen. If he wasn't coming in the door, he was going out. I think he was probably going out."

"Pups said that when she got here, Hennessey called out to her to come in. She didn't know his voice anyway, so she assumed it was him. But she didn't hear a gunshot or the sound of someone falling, so he was obviously dead already, and it was someone else calling to her."

Laurie nods. "If it happened the way she said, then it's possible that when she came in here, the killer went out the front."

"If," I say.

She smiles. As an ex-cop, it's her instinct to disbelieve the accused—the opposite of the way a defense attorney has to think. She's working on it, but it's hard to change old habits. She continues. "It's more likely he went out the back."

We walk to the back door and look out. The small backyard is adjacent to the yards of the houses next door on either side and those of the houses on the block behind us. Behind those houses is Route 20, also known as McLean Boulevard.

"In the dark, it would be easy to get away through here," I say. "And the killer could have a car parked on that street. He could be on the highway in twenty seconds."

She nods. "No question." Then, "I assume nothing was stolen?"

I shrug. "Not sure, but I doubt it. The phone call means the purpose of the killing was not to rob the house but, rather, to implicate Pups."

Once we get the discovery, we'll be able to understand things better for having been here, but right now there's little more to learn.

So we leave. Speaking for myself, I find leaving a murder scene to be preferable to arriving at one.

**W**e've got to go after this from a number of directions simultaneously," I say.

I'm looking around my office conference table, which is really two small wooden tables butted up against each other. It seems fitting; somehow an expensive, ornate conference table in an office one floor above a fruit stand might seem a bit much.

I was in this office on Van Houten Street before I inherited a fortune and then added to my bank account with lucrative cases. I haven't moved for four reasons. One, it just feels like a lot of trouble. Two, I'm comfortable here. Three, moving would make me feel like I was going to continue being an active lawyer, and I don't want to come close to admitting that. And, four, I really like fruit.

The team is all here. In addition to Hike, Laurie, and me, there's Sam Willis, my accountant, who goes into a phone booth and changes into Sam Willis, computer superhero, when we have a case. Sam can hack into anything, and we frequently use that mostly illegal skill to our advantage.

Then there's Edna, my less than hardworking assistant. Edna has perfected a new form of retirement: she does pretty much no work at all but continues to draw a weekly check. Nice nonwork if you can get it.

Willie is here also. He has no official role on the team, but he's always available to help. Willie is fearless, totally reliable, and, as a martial arts expert, is one of the most dangerous people I have ever been around. Of course, that makes him the second most dangerous person on the team.

When it comes to scary and deadly, Marcus Clark makes Willie look like Cinderella. He's a very competent investigator, but we more often use him for his amazing physical skills. Marcus has literally saved my life on a number of occasions and has nearly scared me to death on others. He and Laurie get along great, so he reports in to her. He's a man of very few words, none of them intelligible.

"First of all, we investigate it like we would any murder," I say. "We need to learn everything we can about the victim, Randy Hennessey. What was his job, who were his friends, why did he complain about the dogs, why was he a target, and who had reason to kill him?"

I continue. "At this point, Pups is only accused of the Hennessey murder, but we have to broaden our scope beyond it. The same gun that killed Hennessey killed Jake Boyer and Little Tiny Parker in front of that restaurant eighteen months ago. It is simply not possible that it is a coincidence; somehow, those murders are connected to Hennessey.

"So for the time being, we need to assume that Jake Boyer was the target back then, not Parker. This was not a drive-by shooting of a gang member; it was a targeted assassination of our client's husband. We've got to find out why he was killed, who had reason to kill him, and what the hell his connection is to Hennessey."

"What does our client say about it?" Hike asks.

"She was stunned when I told her and couldn't imagine a connection. Hopefully when she digests it and has time to think, she'll come up with ideas that we can look into. Hike, when will we start getting the discovery?"

"I told Tressel that if the material doesn't start flowing by tomorrow morning, he'll have to explain why to the judge. I reminded him that he agreed to expedite the trial, which means expediting the preparation."

"Good. Once we get the forensics linking the gun to the shooting a year and a half ago, we'll request all the evidence from that case. There will be a truckload of it, but most will be focused on Little Tiny Parker, since he was thought to be the target."

"What have you got for me?" Sam asks. He's the one person in the room who is delighted that we have a case. He finds the whole thing exciting, and I guess compared with his day-to-day accounting work, it is. But Sam is chomping at the bit to move from the computer side to what he calls "working the streets." Sam, I'm afraid to admit, wants to shoot people. I think he only wants to shoot bad people, but you never know.

"Don't know yet, Sam, but there will be plenty. There always is."

I divide up the responsibilities so that I'll look into the

killings from eighteen months ago, while Laurie and Marcus can dig into Hennessey's life. I'm not sure which will take more manpower, but we can revisit it if we need to.

The meeting breaks up, and I drive with Willie down to the Tara Foundation to see how Pups's dogs are doing. He assures me that they're fine, but she's going to ask me when I talk to her—she always does—and I want to be able to say that I saw them.

The mother and puppies are at the Tara Foundation building in Haledon, so we head down there. Willie and Sondra are keeping Pups's dog, Puddles, at their home, but she spends the days with them at the foundation.

There is a small school bus in the parking lot when we get there, and I realize that today is the day that kids from the local grammar school spend a couple of hours at the foundation. It's something that Willie agreed to do; the ten-year-olds interact with the dogs and help take care of them. The school hierarchy thinks that it teaches them good values, and I have to say I agree.

When we get in, I see that the puppies, who give the word "adorable" new meaning, are surrounded by all the kids—actually, all but one: a little girl is sitting on a chair with Puddles in her lap. She's gently scratching Puddles's stomach, and the dog is loving every second of it.

I go over there and ask the girl her name.

"Micaela Reasoner," she says.

"Hi, Micaela. I've got a feeling you like Puddles?"

"I LOVE Puddles," she says. "She's my favorite."

"Do you have a dog at home?"

"No. I have a fish."

She says it in a way that indicates she's not a big fish fan, probably because a fish doesn't react as well when you sit on a chair with it and scratch its stomach.

I walk over to the mother and puppy area, where the other kids are doing their doting. Then I ask Sondra how it's going.

"Great," she says. "We've probably had twenty people in wanting to adopt these puppies. But we're going to hold on to them for at least a few more weeks, until they're more grown."

"What about the mother?"

"There won't be any problem placing her either."

I always enjoy my time at the foundation, and this time hasn't been any different. Good things happen here, and for the right reason.

Unfortunately, it's time to go back to real life.

**T**here just isn't anyone who would have wanted to kill Jake," Pups says.

"I've thought about it, and it's not possible. Jake never hurt a fly."

I'm not surprised to hear Pups say this, for a couple of reasons. First of all, it's a natural reaction for a spouse. To believe that someone wanted to kill her husband, she would have to tacitly acknowledge that he had given a person a reason to hate him, justified or not.

Secondly, at the time of the shooting, to my knowledge she never expressed the belief that Jake might have been a target. If she thought he was, I would think she would have told the police.

"Did the police at the time ever mention that they thought Jake could have been the intended victim?"

She shakes her head. "No, just the opposite. They made it clear they considered him an innocent victim. Wrong place, wrong time."

"Tell me about Jake," I say.

"What do you want to know?"

"Whatever you think is worth telling me," I say, but I prompt her. "How long were you married?"

"Twenty-two years."

"Was he married before?"

She nods. "Yes. Twice."

"Any children?"

"He had one son with his first wife, but he never saw him."

"Why not?"

She shrugs. "Bunch of reasons. Geography, for one. They lived in upstate New York. But the ex-wife didn't handle the divorce well, and she turned the kid against him. Then I heard he started up with drugs, but Jake didn't talk about it much. He had walled off that part of his life. But he said one thing that made me know how much it hurt him."

"What's that?"

"Well, you know Jake and I have always been Mets fans. Jake really got me into it. Well, Jake told me his son pitched in high school, and he was really good. But one day Jake got a phone call, and it upset him. He wouldn't tell me what happened. All he said after the call was that he thought his son was going to be Jerry Koosman, and he wound up being Doc Gooden."

I certainly know what she's saying. Koosman was a terrific left-handed pitcher for the Mets. Gooden was a right-hander destined for greatness, but he destroyed his career and almost his life by getting involved with drugs.

"What did Jake do for a living?"

"For the last ten years of his life, nothing," she says. "Before that, he created software for computers. Medical stuff. Then he went into real estate."

"What kind of real estate?"

"Land. He owns a lot of it." She corrects herself. "Now I own a lot of it."

She starts coughing, so I wait for her to finish. Either she's coughing more lately or I'm just noticing it more because of my knowledge of her disease. "So he left you with a lot of money?"

She frowns. "Yeah, I can pay your fee."

I hadn't even brought up payment for my services; I just assumed Pups had very little money, while I am loaded. "You don't even know what my fee is," I say.

"Doesn't matter; I can pay it. You should talk to Walter Tillman. He knows more about the estate than I do; he handles the money."

Walter Tillman is a prominent local attorney whose firm does mostly estate planning, real estate, wills, and some corporate stuff. I've met him a few times at charity dinners but certainly don't know him well.

"Walter was Jake's lawyer?" I ask.

She nods. "And mine."

"Have you been managing Jake's real estate?"

She shrugs. "Nothing to manage."

"Why not?"

"Talk to Walter."

"I will, but I'll need you to call him and authorize him to discuss your affairs with me. And I'll also need you to think more about Jake and who might have wanted to hurt him.

Also keep thinking about whether there could be any connection that he might have to Hennessey."

She frowns. "I've been thinking about it. No chance. How are the dogs?"

"I saw them; they're all fine. As soon as they're big enough, we'll adopt them out."

"To good homes," she says, making it sound like a warning.

"Of course; that's what we do."

"And Puddles?" she asks.

"Doing great. When I saw her, she was in the lap of a ten-year-old girl getting her stomach scratched."

That gets the first smile out of Pups. "She loves that." Then, "Get me the hell out of here; I want to see her again."

I love walking Ricky to school.

I'm not sure why. It's not as if it reconnects me to a time with my father, since he worked and wasn't around in the mornings when I left. It's just a really peaceful experience, and it seems right.

Usually I take Tara and Sebastian with us. I hold Tara's leash, and Ricky holds Sebastian's. Sebastian is rather easy to handle; he moves so ponderously that it's like he is constantly making decisions as to whether he should take another step.

But today I've got some work responsibilities, so I take Tara and Sebastian on their walk early, and it's just Ricky and me on the way to school. Laurie had told me that she broached the subject of Ricky's last name with him briefly, but she didn't really get anywhere.

She wants me to try, so that's what I do. "Mom said you mentioned that we all have different last names," I say.

"Yeah."

"Does that bother you?"

"Nah."

"It doesn't?"

"Nah."

"You wouldn't want us to all have the same name?" I ask.

"Sure. That would be cool."

I feel like I'm sinking into parental quicksand. "If we could all have the same last name, what would you want it to be?"

He thinks for a few moments. "My friend Will has a cool last name. Let's do that one."

"Rubenstein?" I ask, sinking deeper.

He nods his approval. "Yeah. Ricky Rubenstein. I like that."

"It doesn't really work like that, Rick. We would need to use a name we already have. We already have plenty of them."

"OK, so let's all be Diaz."

"I've got an idea," I say. "Why don't we talk about this with your mother?"

"Cool."

After I drop Ricky off, I walk back home to get my car. I go into the house to get the keys, and Laurie asks me, "Did you talk to him?"

"I did."

"How did it go?"

"How does Mrs. Laurie Collins Diaz Rubenstein sound?"

"What are you talking about?"

"You should not ask me to talk to a ten-year-old. If it's about anything other than sports, I'm in over my head."

My first stop this morning is Walter Tillman's office. Walter was relieved when I called him yesterday to tell him that

I wanted to talk about Pups. She had already notified him that he was free to discuss her situation with me, but he was more anxious to find out what the hell was going on with her case.

Walter has a four-attorney firm with offices in Fort Lee and Newark, and it's at the Fort Lee office that I go to meet him. The office itself is decorated in "old money expensive"; everything except the receptionist is made out of dark-paneled wood. I'm not sure where they found enough dark trees.

Walter, probably in his midfifties, is good-looking and on his third wife. I saw the current Mrs. Tillman at a charity dinner not long ago; it's a pretty good bet that she was born just in time to celebrate his admission to the bar.

We start by chatting about old times and shared experiences, which takes a very short time, since we really don't have any of either. I let him take the lead, and he asks about the situation with Pups's arrest and what jeopardy she might be facing.

"I'm really just getting into it," I say, truthfully. "But clearly someone was out to set her up for this."

"Why the hell would anyone want to do that?" he asks.

"When we know that, we'll know everything."

He sighs. "I thought I'd seen it all, but this . . ." He doesn't finish the thought; he doesn't have to. "So what can I do for you?"

"I'm trying to learn more about why anyone would have wanted to kill Jake Boyer."

He just about does a double take in surprise. "Kill Jake Boyer? That case is being reopened?"

I don't want to mention the gun evidence, but I say, "They're looking at Pups for that shooting as well. I'm trying to head it off."

"That's ridiculous."

"Agreed. Now as to my question."

He shakes his head. "I'm afraid I can't help you with that. I don't have the slightest idea; he was one of the finest, most decent men I've ever met."

"Tell me about his career."

"Well, I only met him when he moved here, so I didn't know him when he was in the software business. And he had already accumulated most of his real estate."

"Where is it located?"

"All over. Jake had a great deal of money and modest needs. So he would buy up a lot of land, mostly at cheap prices, and just hold on to it."

"Hold on to it for what?" I ask.

"Really just for preservation. Jake was what I would call a quiet environmentalist; he didn't broadcast it. But he wanted his land preserved. There were frequent offers to buy various parcels, but he never considered selling; he said he had more than enough money for him and his wife to live on. The only time he ever got rid of land was when he donated some to become part of a national park in Idaho. But the government had to promise that they would leave it untouched."

"Is there a lot of land?"

"In size, yes. Hell, you could just about fit New Jersey in some of those places he owns. But they're mostly in the middle of nowhere."

"So what has happened to all the land since Pups took over?"

He smiles. "Nothing. She's honored his wishes and would never consider selling any of it. She's had some offers, but she instructs me to say no."

"How much is it all worth?" I ask.

"I'm not really sure; there was never any reason to appraise it. But if I had to guess . . . maybe ten or fifteen million for all of it? There's a lot of acreage, but none of it is in Manhattan, that's for sure."

"What happens to the land and the rest of Jake's estate if she's convicted of murdering Jake?"

He nods. "I've been researching that. She would no longer be entitled to the proceeds of the will. My guess is the son would be in line, if anyone could find him, and if he's still alive. Otherwise, the state would step in and sell everything off for the benefit of the state treasury."

"Do you know where the son is?"

"I don't, but it's possible I have some information in the files. I could have my assistant go through it."

"Might be a good idea, more for you than me," I say.

He nods. "Will do. How is Pups feeling? I've known about her illness for a while."

"Seems OK. Coughing some, but not too bad."

"Some position to be in. Her life is on the line, but it's basically over even if she wins. Makes you wonder why she's bothering to fight."

"Fighters fight," I say.

**T**hey've charged her with her husband's murder," Hike says, when I walk into the office.

"And the murder of the gang kid as well. We just got the notice from the court."

"I'm not surprised," I say, because I'm not. Tressel was holding on to those two additional charges to use in case Pups somehow got acquitted of the Hennessey murder. Now there is nothing to be gained by holding them, since Pups will likely have died before a second trial could take place.

The additional charges and the gun evidence linking the two killings will prejudice the jury against Pups. That's why Tressel wants to use it now. It makes sense for the prosecution, but it makes her case that much tougher for us.

"Any other good news for me?" I ask.

"Actually, yes," he says, surprising me. Not only does Hike never deliver good news, but he usually puts a spin on anything positive to make it seem negative. "We've gotten a good amount of the discovery for both killings."

This is good news on two fronts. Most important, it will give us insight into the prosecution's case, and obviously we need that to prepare an effective defense. The other positive is that reading it will give me something to do. That's one of the first things you learn in law school: doing something is better than doing nothing, as long as you're doing it right.

I focus on the Jake Boyer / Little Tiny Parker killings. There is far more information on that case than the Hennessey murder, because months were spent investigating it. On Hennessey, it's an ongoing investigation in its early stages, so the material is limited.

Once I've brought myself up to date on the actual event itself, I call Laurie. "How'd you like to go to another murder scene?" I ask.

"You sure know how to show a girl a good time."

I drive over and pick her up, and we head to the Bonfire Restaurant, on Market Street. It's an easy place to get to, right near the entrances for Routes 20 and 80. It's also the perfect place for this type of drive-by assassination, since the shooter's car could easily slip onto one of the highways and be far away from the scene in minutes.

The Bonfire is the place where we would go on Friday and Saturday nights when we were in high school. If we didn't have a date, we'd go there to hang out with friends. If we did have a date, we'd go there to show her off to our friends. I was most often in no-date mode.

It's not at all crowded when we get there now, since the lunch crowd has mostly left. That doesn't matter to us either way; we have no intention of going in. All the action took place outside.

I point to the entrance. "Boyer and Barnett came out of there about nine thirty. It was a Saturday night, so the place was crowded, and the parking lot must have been filled when they got here. They parked around the corner that way."

"Who drove?" Laurie asks.

"Boyer."

We walk the path that they walked that last night. Laurie points to a street lamp. "The area was lit well enough, unless they've put that in since." She then touches some rust on the pole and says, "Doesn't appear that they have."

"And witnesses said the car almost came to a stop when the shots were fired. With this light, at this distance, it wouldn't exactly take a crack shot to hit the target."

She nods. "I wonder if the shooter deliberately hit the gang guy to confuse the police."

"If he did, it worked."

She smiles. "You're sure the shooter was a he?"

I return the smile. "That's my working theory."

"I think you're right," she says, surprising me.

"Why?"

"Because Pups was his wife; she'd know where he'd be most of the time, and it would usually be in places more vulnerable and less public than this. She didn't have a history of this kind of shooting."

"Glad to hear you've come over to the side of truth and justice and you believe in our client's innocence. Besides, she had an ironclad alibi: she was playing bridge with some friends."

"Obviously, she could have paid to have it done. Especially since you learned he was worth a lot of money."

"Ye of little faith," I say.

"I'm going to have Marcus check into Little Tiny Parker and find out what his friends think," she says. "When a gang member is shot, it's a good bet that his fellow members have a good idea who did it. And they wouldn't be likely to share that information with the police; it's more common that they'd get their own revenge."

"Good idea," I say. "And I'll ask Sam to research online whether there were any follow-up shootings that could have been related. But I think we're going to come up empty; I think Jake Boyer was the target."

**T**he local media is in an uproar.

It's just been made public that Pups is also being charged with the death of her husband and Little Tiny Parker, and it's all anyone is talking about.

Before, while it was obviously a serious murder case, there was still an element of quaintness to it, probably because of the puppy connection. But now it's turned Pups into a borderline serial killer, and the importance of the case, at least in the media's eyes, has exploded.

David Barnett is therefore not at all surprised when I call him and tell him I want to meet. But he's not happy about it. "I know what's going on," he says, "But I really don't want to go back in time. At least not to that night."

"One way or another, you're going to have to, probably more than once. I'll try to make it as painless as possible."

He sighs. "OK. Let's grab a cup of coffee."

When someone tells you that they want to "grab" coffee or lunch or whatever, it means they aren't planning to spend a lot of time with you. "Grab" is the verbal equivalent of taking out and holding car keys; it's a sure sign that they're looking to make a quick getaway.

I consent to the grabbing, and we agree to meet at a diner on Route 46. It's late morning but prelunch, so the place is mostly empty. Barnett's not there when I arrive, although I have no idea what he looks like.

I look around at anyone who might be alone and waiting for me, but unless Barnett is disguised as a sixty-year-old African American woman, then I've arrived before him.

It's twenty minutes and two cups of coffee before he finally arrives. He's dressed in an expensive suit, which is under an even more expensive overcoat. There's fur on the collar, but rather than ask, I'm just going to hope it's not real.

He doesn't apologize for being late but does offer a handshake and a smile. He pretends to shiver and says, "Cold out there."

"Are you dreaming of a white Christmas?" I ask.

He shrugs. "I don't really give a shit; I'm going to be in Hawaii."

He signals to the waitress for a cup of coffee, and I assume that when she brings it over, he's going to grab it.

"So you want to talk about that night," he says. "The worst night of my life, bar none."

"Let's start with you telling me what happened from the time you left the restaurant," I say.

He nods. "Not much to tell. We walked around the corner to his car. He opened it electronically with his key, and I remember that there were some unsavory-looking guys around, gang types, so I wanted him to hurry up. Once he did, I opened the passenger door and started to get in. He wasn't as quick about it, which is probably why I'm here and he's not."

"Did you see the shooter's car?"

"I think so, but I couldn't identify it in any way. I also heard it, and then I heard the gunshots and the screaming."

"What did you do?"

"I got out of the car, which in retrospect wasn't that smart. I saw some of the gang kids hiding behind cars, so I did the same. When they got up, I did. The police were there in no time."

"When you heard the report today that the police think Boyer might have been the target, did that surprise you?"

He thinks for a moment. "Definitely. Partly because I had been told for so long that he wasn't. But also partly because he just wasn't the type someone would want to kill. It's hard to explain, but he was like a gentle soul. You just wouldn't associate him with violence; it doesn't compute. At least that was my impression of him."

"Were you and he friends?"

He shakes his head. "Not really friends, but we were business associates of a sort, and we were friendly."

"Were you having dinner with him about a business matter?"

"Yes. I was making an offer to buy a parcel of land he had in Ohio. A client of mine wanted to build apartment buildings on it."

"You're in real estate?" I ask.

"I am. I buy and sell it for myself and for my clients."

"Were you successful in convincing him to sell?"

He smiles. "Not even close. Once he heard that trees would have to be cut down, he wasn't interested. Didn't even want to hear how much my client was offering." He laughs at the memory.

"What's so funny?"

"I remember I asked him if he had other offers, and he said, 'I hope not.' That's not something I heard very often."

"So, bottom line, you've felt since that day that you guys were just in the wrong place at the wrong time?"

He nods. "Yes, which was a weird feeling. At first, it was like, 'There but for the grace of God' and 'Boy, that puts things into perspective.' But those things kind of fade, and you just put it behind you and move on. I'm not sure how I'm going to react to this new situation, that there was someone out there waiting to kill the person I was having dinner with."

"Have you ever given any thought to the possibility that you were the target?"

"No."

"Why not?"

"Because I'm still breathing."

I nod. "Makes sense. Well, it's a story you'll be able to tell your grandkids."

"I'm not married."

"Then you can tell somebody else's grandkids."

It's time for a talk with Tara.

Very often, when I need to step back and look at the big picture of a case, I do it by taking Tara for a walk and talking it out. She doesn't actually answer me—after all, she's a dog—but she's insightful and a very good listener. And she almost never laughs at me.

I also take Sebastian with us, but he really isn't of much value when it comes to matters involving the criminal justice system. I take him because I know he enjoys the walks and because if I don't take him out, I'm afraid he might piss in the house.

"Tara, when people get set up, they get set up for a reason," I say, and since she doesn't quarrel with my point of view, I continue. "And when murders are involved, it's usually a damned serious reason. Murders can be irrational and sudden and done in the moment; but frame-ups are carefully planned."

Again, she doesn't answer, which is just as well, because some other dog walkers have appeared near us. Since I don't want to look like a nutcase, I'm going to have to telepathically communicate my thoughts to Tara for the duration of the walk.

Hennessey was killed and Pups framed not because she's a pain in the ass or because her dogs barked or because she turned away a potential puppy adopter. That much I know. Unfortunately, among the things I don't know is who did it and why they did it.

Which means I know nothing.

It's not like Pups has been out there living the fast life. She's been basically a hermit for as long as I've known her, even when Jake was alive. She mostly stays at home and takes care of her puppies.

Ironically, the evidence that the same gun was involved in both murders, while making the case against Pups infinitely more difficult for the defense, also makes me more convinced of her innocence.

I believed Pups when she said she didn't kill Hennessey; I have never known her not to be straight. But if generally truth-telling people are ever going to lie, then a prime time would be when creating an alibi for a murder.

But I simply do not believe that Pups killed her husband; from what I know, it makes no sense to me. She didn't run off afterward with someone else or change her lifestyle in any way. And I certainly don't believe she'd be dumb enough to hang on to the gun, only to resurrect it for another murder and then leave it where it could be found.

There are two areas of inquiry that we need to focus on, and the first is Hennessey. Pups swears that neither she nor

Jake had any connection to him, that the only reason she knew he existed was because he filed the complaint with the zoning board.

The zoning board was prohibited by law from telling her who filed the complaint, but Hennessey had mentioned it to some neighbors, possibly as a way of recruiting them to his cause. But all the other neighbors had long been fine with what Pups was doing, so instead three of them told her that Hennessey had filed the complaint. When she confronted him with it, he made a halfhearted denial, but it never seemed to be about anything other than the dogs.

The other area to which we have to pay attention is money. Pups has a lot of it, and it could be that someone wants a shot at it. I don't know how her being convicted of murder would help them get it, though. It's not like she has any heirs, and, if she did, she's not going to be around much longer, anyway.

An heir, like maybe Jake's estranged son, could just as easily show up and claim the inheritance after she has died. If someone has meticulously planned this out, they would likely have learned about her illness.

But the most difficult question is, If someone were going to frame Pups for Jake's murder, why wait a year and a half to do it?

I get back to the house and thank Tara for her time. She hasn't solved the case for me, but she's helped me frame it. And Sebastian did his part; he pissed outside.

Laurie gives me an update on what she and Marcus have found out about Hennessey. "He was no Boy Scout," she says.

"But we haven't found anything to tie him to either of the Boyers."

I decide to latch on to the positive part of what she said, the reference to his not being a Boy Scout, and ask her to fill me in.

"He's had a couple of drug arrests, but for using, not distribution. He was also arrested on a breaking and entering, but the charge was dismissed. I'm trying to find out why, but it's likely lack of evidence."

"Any family?"

She nods. "Yes. A wife and two small kids, living in Hackensack. He seems to have bailed out on them a few months ago, which is when he moved into the house across from Pups. I don't know if he walked or was pushed, but I have the wife's contact information. We could talk to her."

"Where did he live eighteen months ago, when Jake was killed?"

"Camden. He was a carpet salesman. Lost his job, and then one opened up in a store on Route Seventeen. So he took it, lasted a year, and then lost that one too. No evidence that he's been working since."

"We should talk to the wife," I say.

"We? Meaning you and me?"

"Yes. I don't always do that well talking to women."

"I've noticed that," she says.

**T**eresa Hennessey greets us at the door in her nurse's uniform.

The first thing she does, after inviting us in, is to apologize for that fact. "I'm sorry . . . I just got home from work about a half hour ago," she says. "And with the kids . . . I haven't had a chance to change."

She points to her two toddlers sitting in front of the television, one on each side of a black Lab, who seems as into the cartoons as the kids. I'm not a good judge of kids' ages, but these are probably two or three years old. I'm a pretty good judge of dogs' ages, and the white face on this one makes it a very good bet that he's older than the two kids combined.

The kids are eating with their hands from bowls in front of them. It looks like dry Froot Loops, and they are so intent on the televised cartoons that half the Froot Loops are winding up on the floor. The dog happily does the cleanup work.

The best way to describe the house is "lived-in." It's small and sparsely furnished, and the carpet is fraying. This is a woman and family that is barely getting by.

"Absolutely nothing to apologize for," Laurie says. "We appreciate your seeing us, and we're very sorry for your loss."

Teresa just nods without saying anything. It's hard to say what she feels about the size of that loss.

"How are your children doing?" I ask.

"You mean about Randy? I haven't told them yet. They may not even know who I'm talking about. Even when we were together, Randy wasn't around much. Saying he was an absentee father might be giving him too much credit."

We walk over and sit down at a table in the next room, but Teresa is able to maintain a sightline to the children. "Can I get you coffee? Tea?"

We both decline, and Laurie says, "As I told you, we're representing the woman accused of killing your husband."

Teresa nods. "I know."

"We believe that they have the wrong person, and we want to make sure that the real killer is caught and punished."

"I understand."

"Can you think of anyone who would have had a reason to kill your husband?"

"Randall was not the man I married," she says. "We talked about raising a family together; I really thought he was going to be an outstanding father. Then he lost his job, and nothing seemed to go right for him. And he just withdrew; it was like he couldn't handle that he was unable to be exactly what we wanted and needed."

We don't say anything; we just listen as she continues.

"Then he started using drugs; that seemed to come out of

nowhere. Maybe he was doing it before and I didn't notice, or maybe he stopped caring about what I knew and what I didn't. But he was doing it in the house, and one day I left him with the kids, and when I came home, he was completely out of it. So I threw him out."

"This was three months ago?" Laurie asks.

She shakes her head. "No, more like six months ago. He came back . . . he promised to change, but it didn't work. We both knew it, and then he left on his own. Never told me; just took off."

"I'm sorry," Laurie says. "This must be so difficult."

She nods. "It is, but we're getting by. I'm only able to get part-time work so far down at the hospital, but there's talk that something will open up soon. Right now, my biggest worry is how to get them toys for Christmas."

Then, as if she shakes herself out of her own thoughts, Teresa says, "But you're not here to listen to my troubles. The short answer to your question is that I don't know anybody who ever posed a threat to Randy, other than himself. But if he was taking drugs, then he was getting them from somewhere. Maybe he didn't pay? I really have no idea. I wish I could help you."

We gently probe a bit longer but get nowhere. When an argument starts in the other room between the two kids over what to watch on TV, she goes to deal with it and we prepare to make our exit.

Teresa joins us at the door and says, "Sorry about that. They're a handful."

"Your dog seems to take it in stride."

She nods. "He's great with them; he actually calms them down. That's one thing I have to thank Randy for."

"What do you mean?" Laurie asks.

"The dog showed up at our door one day, looking ragged and without a tag. We posted signs, but no one claimed him. Randy couldn't bear to take him to the shelter."

I'm thinking that Randy's attitude toward dogs changed somewhat over time, but I don't mention it. Instead, we just thank her for her time and leave.

Once we're outside, Laurie says, "She has got all she can handle."

I nod. "Merry Christmas." Once we're in the car, I say, "I've got an idea."

"Andy Carpenter, here to save the world."

I don't know how she knows me so well. "Not saving the world, but in this case we can make it a very little bit better."

She smiles. "How much better?"

I've got to be careful giving this number. It needs to be high enough to be significant, but not too high that Laurie thinks it's overdoing it. "Two fifty?"

"Apiece?"

"That would be my preference," I say. "But I defer to you."

She smiles. "Why not? Go for it."

We head for the Toys"R"Us in Paramus, and I go in and buy a five-hundred-dollar gift certificate. It comes in a little envelope, and Laurie writes Teresa on it. We don't sign it, though I would imagine Teresa will have an idea whom it came from.

Once we're back in the car, I call Sam Willis, who answers on the first ring with, "Got something for me?"

"Yes, I do. Can you check into the finances of Randy Hennessey?"

"Sure. Anything in particular you're looking for?"

"Just general stuff. Bank accounts, investments, that kind of thing." I could get this information through a court-ordered subpoena, but Sam can perform his hacking miracles much faster.

When I get off the phone, Laurie asks, "Was that for the case?"

I shrug. "You never know. But if he's got anything, Teresa should get it, and she might not be aware of it."

We drive back to Teresa's house, and Laurie slips the envelope under the door. As we're leaving, Laurie says, "Well, at least we accomplished something."

**W**e've been assuming that Jake was the target in the shooting at the Bonfire.

It makes sense, simply because of the fact that the same gun killed Hennessey. But the police had come to a different conclusion back then, so it would be nice to be sure that we're right. Because if we're wrong, then we're wasting a lot of man and woman hours on a wild goose chase.

According to the discovery and contemporaneous news articles, unlucky Little Tiny Parker was a member of a street gang called the Bloodz. I assume the misspelling is intentional, maybe designed to separate them from other, more literate, Bloods.

Laurie has had Marcus checking into the gang, and he's come back with the information that the leader is named Big Tiny Parker. My keen detecting instincts tell me that it's not a coincidence that there are, or at least were, two Tiny Parkers in the same gang, distinguished only by their different size designations. Since Little Tiny was 250 pounds, Big Tiny must be the size of a side-by-side refrigerator/freezer. That is, unless the Bloodz are heavily into irony, in which case Big Tiny probably looks like Mary Lou Retton.

"Marcus said Big Tiny will talk to you," Laurie tells me.

"Wonderful," I say. "It's at the top of my bucket list. Hopefully, he'll bring Enormous Tiny with him also."

"Tonight?" she asks.

"Why not?"

Laurie calls Marcus, and he says he'll pick me up at eight o'clock. It gives me time to have dinner with Laurie and Ricky.

While we're eating, Ricky asks me if I want to play a game of Madden Football with him later. We've played maybe ten or twelve games so far, and he's dominated every one of them. "I can't, Rick," I say. "I've got to go see a very large friend."

I go outside at 7:59 and forty-five seconds, knowing that Marcus will pull up fifteen seconds after that. You can set your clock by Marcus; I don't know how he does it.

We drive to a bar in a depressed area of downtown Paterson. Marcus almost never talks, and this drive is no exception. I make a halfhearted effort at conversation with, "Got any plans for the holidays?" and his response is "Nunh." Short and to the point.

As we near the place, I ask if he's sure that Big Tiny will talk to us. "Yunh," he says, adding a little nod for emphasis. There are cars on the street, so we have to park down the block, in front of a diner. We get out and walk to the bar, which takes less than a minute.

There are three very large, rather disagreeable-looking people standing near the door of the bar. I'm not liking this situation, though I'd like it a hell of a lot less if I wasn't with Marcus. Of course, if I wasn't with Marcus, I'd be home watching the Knicks game.

As we walk toward the door, the three guys move in front of it, blocking our way. Marcus doesn't say anything, so I jump in. "We're here to talk to Big Tiny."

"Is that right?" the middle guy says. "What about?"

"We have an appointment."

That gets a sort of laugh-cackle out of Middle Guy. He moves his arm slightly, and the next thing I know, there is an open knife in his hand. "You got an appointment? Is that what you got? Well, I got one of these."

This is usually the part where Marcus disables the three of them, and I step gingerly over their prone bodies and enter the establishment in triumph. But this time he's not doing anything. "Marcus, did you clear this ahead of time?" I ask.

He doesn't say anything, and after a few moments lightly takes my arm and pulls me away from the bar. We start walking back toward the car. As much as I'm delighted to have exited that confrontation without shedding any blood, backing down like this is very uncharacteristic of Marcus. Maybe he made an assessment that he wouldn't prevail and wisely retreated. If so, that would be the first time.

We get back to the car, and I take out the keys to unlock it, but Marcus says, "Nunh." Then, in an absolute lengthy soliloquy, he points to the diner and says "In there."

"You want me to go in there?"

"Yunh."

"Are we going to have dinner?"

He just points again, and I go in alone. I sit at a table and order coffee as I see Marcus heading back toward the bar. I'm feeling guilty that he's going it alone, but I'd feel worse if I was with him. Apparently, the situation was such that he felt he couldn't handle it and protect me at the same time; I like the way the guy thinks.

Fifteen minutes go by, and they feel like a hundred. Even though past history has told me that I shouldn't be, I'm worried about Marcus. There were three of those guys, and they were probably all armed, and there might have been more in the bar. I decide that I'll wait five more minutes and then call the police.

Two minutes before my self-imposed deadline, Marcus comes back. He's with a person who truly would make Little Tiny look like Little Tiny. This guy, who I assume is Big Tiny, has got to be 320 pounds, and he's not even particularly fat. He could literally have me for lunch, with room for dessert.

They enter, and Marcus points toward my table, so they take the two chairs opposite me. I have no idea how the relatively flimsy chair is able to hold "Big Tiny," but it manages to do so.

Big Tiny looks sullen and defeated, and all he says is, "So talk."

I know I should get this over with, but I can't help myself. "What happened to those three guys?" I ask, since I know I'll never get the information out of Marcus.

"You don't want to know," he says.

"Marcus didn't kill them, did he?"

Suddenly, Big Tiny's face lights up in recognition. "That's Marcus Clark?"

"Yes."

"Man, I heard about him, but I didn't believe it. Now I believe it."

"Just to confirm, and not to nitpick this, but he didn't kill them, did he?"

"Nah, but they ain't gonna be no good for me for a while, that's for damn sure."

"Sorry, but they brought it on themselves. Nobody messes with me and Marcus; if I was there, it would have been worse," I say. "And even though you may not believe this, we are all on the same side here."

"Bullshit."

"It's the truth. So let's talk about your brother."

**W**hat the hell you want to know about my brother?"

Big Tiny stiffens at the mere mention of his brother; his death is obviously still a sore point for him. He half stands up, and the only purpose for standing would be to either leave or make a physical move at me. But Big Tiny didn't get to be where he is by being a dummy, and he instantly realizes that Marcus's presence makes either of those choices impossible. Since he wants to remain the only living Tiny, he sits back down.

"We want to know who killed him," I say.

"If I knew that, he'd be a dead man. Nobody could stop me, not even Mr. Marcus here."

"The police thought it was a gangland shooting."

"The police don't know shit."

"Why do you say that?"

"You think I don't have people on the street? Somebody in another gang orders breakfast, I know how they take their eggs. You understand?"

"I think so. You have informants that supply you with information about other gangs, including their preferences regarding eggs and, I assume, pancakes and cereal."

Big Tiny turns to Marcus. "Man, whatever he's paying you, it ain't enough. Come work for me; we'll take over the damn world."

Marcus doesn't respond, which might make Big Tiny think that he's pondering the proposal. He's not; Marcus never responds. At least I hope he's not. If Marcus were to switch sides, it would cause a significant shift in the balance of power, generally, and at this table, specifically.

"So all the information you gathered told you it wasn't a gang killing?"

"That's right."

"What about someone else who might have had a grudge against your brother? For whatever reason, maybe an argument over a girl?"

"No chance. Everybody liked him."

Big Tiny's assessment of his brother's likeability doesn't completely jibe with his criminal record, but that could just be a case of blind brotherly love. "He had arrests for assault," I say. "Maybe one of his victims was getting revenge?"

"Whoever did would know they'd have to deal with me. I'm telling you, there is no chance. Now, we done here?"

I've got nothing else to ask him, so I say, "Yeah, we're done."

Big Tiny stands up, and in doing so towers over us; the man is huge. He says, "If you guys are really trying to find out who killed my brother and you need my help, just ask. Like I told you, I got guys on the street. You got a pen?"

I hand him one and he takes out a small piece of paper, then writes a phone number on it. "You want to reach me, that's my private number. I don't want you showing up at my office no more." Then he turns to Marcus and says, "Man, you . . . ," and then seems unsure how to finish the sentence, so he just turns and leaves.

I didn't get any information out of this encounter, which in itself is a significant piece of information. The police, while considering Little Tiny to have been the target, came up with no suspects. His highly motivated older brother, no doubt telling the truth when he said he was well tied in to street information, came up empty as well.

It tends to confirm my existing theory that the killer was after Jake. I don't have to prove the theory to use it as my operating assumption, so it will help me keep focus in the investigation.

Unfortunately, I don't have to prove it to a jury either, because the prosecution will be making the same argument. They will agree that Little Tiny was not the target but, rather, that the intended victim was Jake Boyer. It will be the center-piece of their case.

They will tell the jury that the killer was the person who had the murder weapon, his wife and my client, Pups. Then, having murdered once and gotten away with it, she had no qualms about killing a person who infuriated her eighteen months later, Randy Hennessey.

After all, what did she have to lose? She knew she was dying, anyway.

I ask Marcus if he wants to get something to eat while we're here, and I'm glad he doesn't. There's always the chance that Big Tiny might be back with some big friends, seeking revenge.

We get in my car and drive off, passing the bar where we had our confrontation. There's a bit of traffic, caused by the presence of an ambulance, with another ambulance pulling away.

"Marcus, is that . . . never mind."

**H**e used three names, sometimes four, on a regular basis.

He used only one name on each project, regardless of the complexity, or how much was involved. It helped him keep things straight. He never used his own name, and sometimes he couldn't be sure that he really had one anymore.

The one he used on this project, from the very beginning, was Caffey. It was one of his favorites, though he wasn't sure why. It sounded important, and it sounded tough. Which was good, because he was important, and he was tough.

He'd been back east for less than two weeks, and he hadn't been called on to do much, just to follow that lawyer, Carpenter. Not exactly tough work, but not particularly exciting or challenging either. The previous times he'd been called here, he'd had to kill people. First, the two guys outside the restaurant, and then that loser Hennessey.

It didn't much matter to Caffey if he followed someone or killed them. He got paid the same; he was on the clock, and it was a really expensive clock at that.

So he followed Carpenter, and every other day he called one of his employers and reported Carpenter's movements. His impression was that Carpenter was flailing around, covering bases but not making any real progress. But he left that out of his reports; all his employers wanted were the facts, not opinion. Which was fine with Caffey; for what these people were paying, they could have whatever the hell they wanted.

So far, each time he reported in, the response was the same: just keep following Carpenter and keep reporting those movements.

Caffey had been down this road before, and his hunch was that one of these times, the orders would be to follow Carpenter and kill him.

Whatever.

**R**andy Hennessey came into some money," Sam says.

He's come to my office to tell me about it, which is not a big hardship, since his accounting office is just down the hall.

Two questions come to mind, so I might as well ask both of them at once. "When, and how much?"

"Fifteen thousand on November twelfth and another ten thousand five days later."

I can check this to confirm, but I think that those two dates are around the time he filed the complaints about Pups with the zoning board. If I had to guess, payment number 1 came before, and payment number 2 came after.

"Do we know where the money came from?"

He nods. "Sort of. It was wired from an account registered to the Committee for a Better America, set up at one of those online banks."

"Any way to find out who's on the committee?"

"No one; it's all bull. The name is just a front. The people set up as the officers don't exist. Those banks aren't exactly rigid in setting up checking accounts; I'm sure the documentation that was used was fake."

"Can you get copies of those documents?" I ask.

"I'm not sure; I can try, but they have to have been entered online. But I know what they say, and they're not going to help you any."

"Get whatever you can, Sam, just in case. Has Hennessey gotten payments like this before?"

"I went back two years, and he's never had more than two grand in his account at any point. Now he has almost twenty-four; he spent a little before he got shot."

"Sam, can you get into Hennessey's phone records, landline, and cell—whatever he had?"

He frowns as if I insulted him. "Of course."

"Good. I want to know everyone he talked to in the period before his death. Go back a couple of months."

"No problem."

"Thanks, Sam. This is a big help."

"I'm here to serve."

I call Hike, and I ask him to get a subpoena to legally retrieve the same records of Hennessey's that Sam just got illegally. I also tell him to get in touch with Teresa Hennessey, tell her about this money, and help her do whatever is legally necessary to allow her to get her hands on it.

Then I call Laurie and tell her what Sam has learned.

"So unless we're dealing with a huge coincidence here, somebody paid Hennessey twenty-five thousand dollars to complain about Pups's dogs?" she asks.

"Sounds a tad suspicious," I say.

"Why do we think they did that?"

"To set Pups up as his enemy so that when he was killed, they would look to her. Hennessey didn't realize that he was signing his own death certificate when he took the money and made the complaint."

"But the zoning board kept it confidential."

"Yes, but Hennessey apparently didn't, and it was probably part of the deal that he made sure the word got out. I'm about to look into that now," I say.

My next call is to Pups, to find out exactly who told her that Hennessey was the one who complained. She gives me three names of neighbors, so I drive over to her street, figuring at least one of them will be home. I get lucky on the first try; a woman named Mary Dixon is there, and she recognizes me because she was at the hearing that overturned the zoning-board decision. She and some of the other neighbors had showed up to support Pups.

She invites me in and immediately expresses a desire to help Pups in any way possible. "That sweet woman would never murder anyone," she says.

"Sweet woman?" I ask, my surprise evident. I have never heard anyone describe Pups that way. "We're talking about the same Pups?"

Mary laughs. "Maybe not sweet in the traditional sense. But if you dig deep enough . . . she's got a sweet soul . . . Anyway, how can I help you?"

"Pups said that you told her Hennessey was the person that complained to the zoning board."

She nods. "I hope I didn't in some way contribute to all this."

"Not at all. But tell me how you found out about it?"

"He told me," Mary says. "And I didn't exactly have to beat it out of him. He told me what he did and said he hoped I'd back him."

"What did you say?"

"That I most certainly would not back him and that I was on Pups's side."

"Did he ask you to keep his role a secret?"

"Not at all. I told him I was going to tell her, and he was fine with it. He seemed to want me to."

"Did you talk about it with the other neighbors?" I ask.

"I sure did, and Hennessey had the same conversation with most of them as he did with me. I hate to talk ill about the dead, but he was not a nice man."

I thank her and leave; there's no reason to talk to any of the other neighbors. I have little doubt that Hennessey was paid to complain about the dogs, and part of his job was to make sure that Pups knew about it.

He certainly did that job well; his complaint was heard, and he did everything but take an ad out in the paper to get Pups angry at him.

So what I know now is that someone murdered Jake Boyer, then waited a year and a half to set Pups up for it. That person, or group of people, then paid twenty-five thousand dollars to Hennessey, who did not realize he'd never live to spend it.

These are serious, deadly, patient people we are dealing with. I just need to find out what they're hoping to accomplish, and then maybe I can find out who they are.

It's got to be about the money.

Pups has a lot of it, and somebody wants to take it from her. It's the only way I can explain this, even though I still have no idea who is trying to do it or how they can possibly pull it off.

Pups doesn't seem to know how much money she has and isn't terribly interested in knowing. Since she referred me to Walter Tillman about it, I decide to call Walter and pump him for more information. Maybe there's something I missed the first time we talked.

My need to call Walter is lessened somewhat when he calls me first. "You were my next call," I say.

"What about?"

"Pups's money."

"She already authorized me to pay whatever bills you submit for your fee."

"Nice to hear, but that's not what I meant. Someone has gone to great pains to get their hands on her money, and I'm trying to figure out who that might be."

"I have no idea what you're talking about, but how can I help?" Tillman asks.

"You prepared her will?"

"I did."

"Who is she leaving her estate to?"

He hesitates, a lawyer's natural reaction when asked to reveal something that might be in confidence.

"She's already authorized you to talk to me," I say. "I can get her to do so again, but I'd rather move this thing along."

"OK," he says. "She's left it to a number of animal rescue organizations all over the country. At last count, I believe there were a hundred and fifty-one of them, and the average amount was, like, a hundred grand each in cash."

I'm thinking, Wow, so I say, "Wow." Then, "That is going to be huge for those groups."

"And that doesn't include the land that Jake owned, which is going to other animal rights groups. That could be worth almost as much. She put a lot of work into researching and choosing the beneficiaries, and then she gave it to me to do due diligence. People in my office spent three weeks talking about Chihuahuas. It's amazingly detailed."

"So let me ask you what happens in the various scenarios. If she is not convicted of killing Jake, the will is executed as per her wishes when she dies?"

"Correct," he says.

"What if she is convicted? What happens upon her death then?" I think I know the answer to this, but it's not my area of the law, so I want to hear him confirm it.

"Legally, whether she is alive or dead wouldn't matter, because once she is convicted, the proceeds she derived from Jake's estate will no longer belong to her. So her will would only direct money she had independently of Jake's estate, which is almost nothing."

"So on a conviction, where does the big money go?" I ask.

"Depends. If another potential heir steps forward, then he or she can claim it and the court would decide. If not, the state steps in and puts the cash in the state treasury. Then they'd sell the land in an orderly fashion and keep those proceeds as well."

"And the only potential heir would be Jake's son?"

"His name is Hank Boyer, and he's the only one I am aware of."

"And he hasn't been heard from in years?"

"That's why I was calling," Tillman says. "I checked through the files like I said I would, and I found some information on him. I was trying to cover all my bases when I prepared Jake's estate, and I got whatever information Jake had. I've got an address, though I don't know if it's still current, and even a photograph."

"Where is the address?"

"You ready? Deadwood, South Dakota."

"That's convenient. Can you scan it all and send it to me? And can you also send me a list of the land holdings and a map of where they are?"

"Sure," Tillman says. "Hopes this helps."

"Not sure how it can, but the more information I have, the better."

"How's the case going?" he asks.

"It's going. Merry Christmas."

**T**oday is "tree decorating day." It's not my favorite day of the year, but it's not the worst either. For instance, I like it more than "root canal day," and "food poisoning day," and "colonoscopy day."

We're doing it late this year, as it's only ten days until Christmas, but I've been so busy that I keep putting it off. Finally, Laurie and Ricky got tired of waiting, so they went out and got the tree without me. Today, we're going to put on the lights and ornaments. Laurie has countless boxes of each; I believe it is the largest privately owned collection in the Western Hemisphere.

We begin by wrapping the lights around the tree, starting at the top. I like to put a lot of distance between the rows of lights so we'll get to the bottom faster. Ricky will take over when we get down to near his height level; it's one of the reasons I wish he would grow more quickly. But Laurie insists on almost no space at all between the rows, so it takes forever to get down there.

Then we start with the ornaments. Laurie and Ricky

disapprove of somewhere between 98 and 100 percent of my placements, so I am given the responsibility of placing the ones in the back of the tree, facing the wall. That way, no one will ever see them.

So I spend the time by myself back there behind the tree, adding the ornaments that will be forever unseen. Of course, that doesn't stop both Laurie and Ricky from occasionally glancing back there and shaking their heads in a silent reprimand at my pathetic efforts.

I finish the back before they're even close to done with their masterpiece, so I head down to the Tara Foundation. This is a particularly busy time of year, since people often want to get dogs as Christmas gifts. We are not enamored of this type of adoption; dogs are not ties or sweaters or tennis racquets.

This year, Willie and Sondra are especially busy, because the puppies are grown enough to be placed in homes. Puppies are a hot ticket, especially in rescue land. People can get a cute little puppy and feel good that they made a rescue; for them, it's the best of both worlds.

We have a waiting lounge at the foundation, and two sets of potential adopters are in there, since Willie and Sondra are seeing other people. I will pitch in and help, but first I want to tell Willie and Sondra that I'm there.

Sandra is in one of the open play areas with a family of four. They are interacting with one of the puppies, and everybody seems to be smiling. Sandra is a very good judge of dog homes; any adoption that she makes, I'm totally happy with.

I tell her that I'm there and will handle one of the waiting families. She talks softly to me, "Why don't you check in on Willie first? I've got a bad feeling about that one."

I've got a good guess what she's talking about. Willie is very protective of these dogs; they are his children. And he can be a tad direct in telling someone they can't adopt one of our dogs; Willie does not have a very good kennel-side manner.

Willie is in one of the offices with a man in his thirties, well dressed with a very expensive overcoat on his arm. There is a puppy near him on the floor, and the way the man is still holding his coat gives me the idea that he has not physically interacted with the dog.

Not a good sign.

I walk in and shake hands with the man, introducing myself.

"Kyle Holt," he says, seemingly pleasant enough.

"Andy's my partner," Willie says. "Why don't you tell him what you just told me?"

Holt seems surprised to have to repeat himself, but says, "I want to get this puppy for my son for Christmas. It's a surprise."

"His wife doesn't even know about it," Willie says. "Big surprise."

I'm afraid I can see where this is going, as Willie continues. "But he wants to know if he can bring it back." He turns to Holt. "What's the word you used? 'Exchange'?"

Holt nods. "Right, in case they don't like it or they think one of the other ones is cuter. And, of course, they might not want one at all. I assume your policy is to take it back?"

Kaboom.

"Here's our policy," Willie says. "You can't have this dog," Willie says. "In fact, our policy is you can't have any one of our dogs."

Holt is clearly taken aback. "Why not? Is there a problem?"

Willie nods. "The problem is that I'm exchanging you for a different adopter, because I don't like you. I'm going to find someone cuter."

Holt doesn't seem to know what to say, which is just as well, because anything he might say is only going to annoy Willie more. And Willie past a certain annoyance point can lead to some volatility.

"Mr. Holt, I don't think this is going to work out," I say. "But thanks for your time, and we at the Tara Foundation hope you have a great holiday."

Holt is smart enough to know that there is nothing that is going to turn this around, so he just shakes his head. "I think I'll take my business elsewhere."

"Good plan," I say, as he leaves.

"Asshole," Willie says, loud enough that the departing Holt can hear it. Holt does not turn around, indicating that, while he may be an asshole, he is no dummy.

"I didn't know you were coming down today," Willie says, once he leaves.

"It's tree-decorating day at home."

"Oh, man, that's the worst," he says. "Sondra uses so many lights there are planes landing on our roof."

"How is it going down here?"

He perks up. "Great. Three puppies left, and the mother is spoken for once the puppies are gone. Great homes."

"You got pictures for Pups?"

"Course," he says. He hands me a bunch of photographs of each dog as he or she went home with its forever family, plus a picture of Puddles, once again being held by Micaela, the young girl who comes by pretty much every day to play with her.

"Thanks. You have time to take a trip with me?"

"On a case? Where to?" he asks.

"South Dakota."

"Where the hell is that?"

"Just south of North Dakota," I say.

"Why are we going there?"

"Because we've got nothing else to do."

**D**an Tressel calls me; it's the first time we've talked since the arraignment.

He reaches me on my cell as I'm on the way to the prison to meet with Pups.

"You want to come in and talk?" he says. "I thought I would have heard from you by now."

"Talk about what?"

"Avoiding a trial. It doesn't do anybody any good."

His offering a plea, regardless of terms, surprises me. It must be coming from above him, because when he says nobody gains from a trial, he's lying. As a prosecutor, a triple-murder conviction is a major plus on a resume, and he wouldn't be giving it up willingly.

"Let's talk on the phone; I doubt we'll have that much to say. What are you offering?"

"She cops to killing her husband and Little Tiny, and we drop the Hennessey hit. She gets twenty to life, although we both know life is going to come first."

"You're using up my cell phone rollover minutes on this?" I ask. "Forget it."

"What are you looking for?"

"An apology from the state and a cash settlement for wrongful arrest. But the apology needs to come from the governor, and it has to be heartfelt. It would be a nice touch if he got choked up."

He laughs. "Music to my ears; I'm going to love this trial. But don't you need to discuss this with your client?"

"I'll be doing that in twenty minutes. You'll hear from me if she's interested, which means you won't hear from me."

We hang up, and, before I get to the prison, I reflect on why he made the offer. The unlikely reason is that there is a weakness in his case—unlikely because I'm pretty confident I would have found it by now.

More probable is that the people above Tressel decided that it would be an expensive waste of money, and somewhat unseemly to boot, to try a dying woman. If she pleads guilty, they accomplish the same thing without the negatives.

There is no chance that Pups will accept the terms, but when I get to the prison, I present them to her, being careful not to show any of my own bias in the process. "Why are you bringing me this crap?" is her delicate response when she hears it.

"Because I'm your lawyer. Crap bringing is part of my job description."

"My answer is no," she says.

I nod. "That's what I told them."

"Good. For a minute there, I was worried about you." She points to a manila envelope I'm holding. "Those are pictures?"

"They are."

Pups coughs a few times; she's been doing that more and more lately. She frowns as if annoyed with herself for doing so, but she never comes close to complaining, and she has every right to. This woman is dying, and instead of living out her days with dignity, she's stuck in a prison cell, awaiting trial for murders I believe she did not commit.

I hand her the envelope, and she opens it and thumbs through the pictures. Most of them are photos that Willie and Sondra took of the puppies with their adoptive families. Pups scrutinizes them carefully, as if she can somehow tell from the photographs whether or not the families are good enough for her puppies.

There are also a few more pictures of Micaela holding and petting Puddles. Pups seems to get emotional when she sees them, but she covers it up quickly. "What's the little girl's name?"

"Micaela Reasoner."

"Tell her that Puddles loves the reverse pet."

"What's the reverse pet?" I ask.

She frowns, as if she's talking to a moron. "When you pet a dog's head, it's not front to back; it's back to front. Neck up to forehead, not forehead down to neck."

"Got it. I'll tell her. You doing OK in here?"

"Yeah, I'm having a blast. What else you got?"

"A question. And I know I've asked you this before, but what do you know about Jake's son, Hank?"

She thinks for a few moments. "Not much more than I said; Jake didn't talk about him at all. I just know that he was a troubled kid, good athlete, dropped out of school, got into trouble, used drugs. His mother turned him against Jake—at least that's what he told me. Then when she died, Jake tried to reach out to him, but the kid wasn't interested. I think he went out west somewhere. Why?"

"Just ticking off the boxes," I say.

"Well, go tick some more boxes; you're not accomplishing anything here. Get me some more pictures, and don't forget to tell Micaela about the reverse pet."

've debated with myself about taking this trip. For one thing, Deadwood, South Dakota, is not that easy to get to from New York. There are no direct flights, so we'll have to switch planes. Then we'll fly to Rapid City, rent a car, and drive the forty-five minutes to Deadwood. In South Dakota's late-December weather, I would think that a forty-five-minute drive could take close to a month.

More important, the possible benefit to our case is not readily apparent. We're trying to find the potential heir to Jake's will, but since Pups has already received the proceeds from that will, the newly found heir would only become eligible if she is convicted of murdering Jake. My job, of course, is to prevent that.

But the state of our case is such that we need to go after any remote chance of finding a breakthrough. My theory is that someone is after Pups's money, and the only candidate that I can come up with is the person that would be in line to get it: Jake's estranged son, Hank Boyer.

It's a long shot. Hank has not been heard from and certainly has made no apparent effort to get any of his father's money. I can't even be sure he knows that his father is dead. It's hard to believe that he is orchestrating this complex plot from Deadwood, South Dakota, but one never knows. Even if I just eliminate him as a possibility, I've made some progress.

It was Laurie's idea for me to bring Willie along. She wants him there to protect me in case of trouble, but she isn't worried enough to suggest that I bring Marcus. She knows that Marcus scares the hell out of me, so this represents a compromise in her mind. Plus, she knows that Willie could handle most things likely to come up.

There is no getting around one simple fact: Laurie doesn't think I can take care of myself in dangerous situations; she would send along a bodyguard if I was attending a meeting of the Camp Fire Girls.

"There is no reason to think that this trip is in any way dangerous," I said, trying to reason with her.

"We know of three murders already," Laurie pointed out. "Willie goes, or I send Marcus. In fact, maybe Marcus is the better idea. You can have all your meals together, play cards . . . maybe you can share a room."

I nodded. "Willie it is."

We're flying from LaGuardia rather than JFK, because it eliminates the need to drive on the always awful Van Wyck Expressway. I know what the history books say, but I still believe that the Donner party got lost on the Van Wyck.

So we take an early morning flight to Chicago O'Hare,

then have a fifty-minute layover for the flight to Rapid City. We're flying first class, because the seats are wider and they warm the peanuts. The other major plus is that, this way, we don't have to fight for overhead-bin room. Since the airlines started charging to check bags, overhead-bin space has become more precious real estate than Rodeo Drive.

There is clearly a rule at O'Hare that, no matter what flight you come in on, your connecting flight must be at a gate as far away as possible. And, since there are member countries of the United Nations smaller than O'Hare, it can be a bit of a hassle.

Willie and I have to run what feels like a marathon to make our connection. When we finally get there, I'm in need of an oxygen tent, and Willie isn't even breathing heavily. It takes me almost until the pilot announces the final descent into Rapid City to stop panting.

We drive to Deadwood, a small community whose downtown consists mostly of hotels, casinos, and stores for tourists to buy souvenirs. Deadwood has pretensions of still being a remnant of the Wild West, and as such has a certain charm. It's set against the Black Hills and Mount Rushmore, so if you like slot machines, incredibly beautiful scenery, and historic, epic mountain carvings of presidents, you could do worse.

It gets dark early this time of year, so Deadwood is lit up when we arrive. Christmas lights are everywhere, and the stores all advertise holiday sales. Deadwood T-shirts: buy one, get one free. You can't beat that.

"You gotta be kidding," Willie says, when we first get out

of the car, though I'm not sure if he means that as a positive or a negative. But he follows that with, "You think there were gunfights in this town?"

I nod. "I reckon."

We check into Cadillac Jack's Gaming Resort, not to be confused with the Bellagio or Venetian. But it's got character of a sort, and a restaurant, and clean rooms, so we should be fine.

Laurie had done some research and learned that Hank Boyer works here as a blackjack dealer, so the first thing I do, even before we have dinner, is head for the blackjack pit. I ask the pit boss if Hank Boyer is on tonight, but he tells me that his shift finished a couple of hours ago, and he won't be back on until ten in the morning.

Willie and I have dinner; it turns out that Cadillac Jack makes a pretty good steak. As we're finishing, I say, "You want to hang out down here for a while or go to sleep?" I don't suggest having a drink, since I rarely drink alcohol, and Willie never does.

I'm asking the question to be nice; it's been a long day, and I'm ready for bed.

He shakes his head. "No, I'm pretty tired, and I want to get up early."

"What for? You bringing in a herd?"

"Nah, I just want to walk around the town."

We start to head upstairs to our rooms, but Willie stops along the way and looks at some Western paraphernalia for sale in the gift shop. He picks up a Western hat and tries it on. "What do you think?" he asks.

"I think you look ridiculous," I say.

So he buys it.

Willie's really into this Western stuff, even though, except for a brief California trip we took together, I think the farthest west he has been before today is Parsippany. If he starts calling me "pardner," I'm going to put him on a plane.

**C**affey had gotten behind Carpenter and his friend in the airport check-in line.

It wasn't completely necessary, because he was sure that he knew where they were going. But Caffey was a perfection-ist and left nothing to chance. If he was 99 percent certain of something, then it was 1 percent short of satisfactory.

So Caffey got close enough to overhear them talking to the ticketing agent, and, once he heard the destination con-firmed, he melted into the background.

As soon as he left the airport, he called his employer. "They're heading for Deadwood," he said.

"What do you mean, 'they'?"

"He took the guy from the dog place with him."

"OK," said the employer.

"You want me to get on a plane? I can pick him up when I get there. We know where he'll be."

"No need. Pick him up again when he gets back."

"You got it."

Click.

I have pancakes for breakfast, and Willie has another steak.

He tells me, with obvious disappointment, that he spent the early morning without seeing a single gunfight.

It's Sunday morning, and there is a sleepy feel to the hotel restaurant and, especially, the casino. Most of the players look like they're still there from last night; the smell of victory is not in the air.

At ten o'clock, we head for the blackjack area, and I'm about to walk over to the pit boss when I see a dealer standing behind a blackjack table. There's little doubt in my mind that it's Hank Boyer. He looks a bit older, but he matches the picture that Walter Tillman gave me.

"Let me do this alone," I say to Willie. "If he runs away, you rustle up a posse."

There's no one playing at Hank's table; he's probably just opened up. I walk over and sit down in a player's seat. I put five twenty-dollar bills on the table, and he counts it out and gives me twenty red chips in return.

He's dealing single-deck blackjack, unlike most of the tables, which deal eight decks out of a "shoe." Single-deck gives players the illusion that they have better odds, because it's easier to count cards, a technique more than frowned on by casinos. But single-deck dealers shuffle so often that they mostly remove this advantage.

Hank holds the deck in his left hand and flings the cards toward me with his right. In single-deck, the player actually picks up and looks at the cards; when they're dealt from a shoe, the player never touches the cards. So in single-deck, the occasional gambler feels more involved.

After a few hands, I ask, "You're Hank Boyer, aren't you?" I already know what the answer is; he matches Tillman's photo, and he has the name Hank on his shirt pocket.

He looks at me suspiciously and says, "Do I know you?"

"We've never met, but I knew your father."

"I don't have a father" is his very cold response.

"My name is Andy Carpenter, and I'd like to talk to you about him."

He doesn't respond, so I add, "I won't take a lot of your time. We flew here from New York to see you, so . . ."

He's been continuing to deal as we talk, but this stops him. "Why the hell did you do that?"

"To talk to you about your father."

He stiffens slightly, but noticeably. "Tell him I don't want to talk to him, I don't want to see him, and I don't want anything to do with him. Nothing's changed."

"I'm sorry," I say, "but something has definitely changed. He passed away eighteen months ago."

Another stiffening, this time more noticeably. "Well, then that's that."

"Not quite," I say. "I really need to talk to you about something important."

He seems about to resist but then sighs. "OK. After I get off. Come to the house. My wife is going to want to hear this, so she might as well get it from the horse's mouth."

Since I'm obviously the horse, he gives me his address, and we agree to meet at his house at seven o'clock this evening. It's a mixed blessing; I was hoping to get on an afternoon flight out of here today, which is obviously not going to happen. But it frees me to watch NFL football all day, which starts at eleven AM out here.

Football in the morning and no gunfights. The Wild West really has become civilized.

I call my bookmaker in New Jersey, Jimmy Rollins, and make some small bets on the games. I have to do it with Jimmy, because one can't bet on a sporting event in South Dakota. You see, they consider gambling immoral or something, and I say that while sitting in one of their gambling casinos.

So Willie and I spend the day in the sports bar, eating, drinking, and watching. It turns out that I have no better betting luck west of the Mississippi, but it's still a very enjoyable, relaxing day.

We get to Hank Boyer's house at exactly seven o'clock. Willie thinks it will go better if he waits in the car, and I'm OK with that.

Hank's wife, Sharon, greets me at the door. It's a modest

house, but very well kept. I introduce myself, and Sharon apologizes for the place being a mess, but if there's the slightest actual evidence of that, I don't see it.

"Hank! Mr. Carpenter is here!"

Hank comes in from the back, wiping what looks like grease off his hands onto a towel. He was probably in his toolshed. I've got to get myself a toolshed, but first I should get some tools. In any event, he doesn't offer to shake hands, which in this case I view as a positive.

Sharon asks me if I want coffee or soda or anything to eat, but I decline it all. The house doesn't seem to have a den, so we sit at the kitchen table. I don't see any evidence of children in the house, and children generally leave plenty of evidence.

"So before I get into who I represent and why I'm here, I want to offer my condolences about your father. Hearing it from a stranger in a casino is not optimal."

"Doesn't matter to me," Hank says.

"Hank . . . ," Sharon says, in what seems to be a gentle admonishment.

"I'm sorry, but my father was dead to me a long time ago. So nothing has changed."

"I understand. For your information, he was killed in a drive-by shooting in Paterson, New Jersey. That's where he lived."

"Oh, my," Sharon says, but Hank remains silent, so I continue.

"Did you know his third wife? Her name is Martha."

"He only had three of them?" Hank asks, not really expecting an answer.

"Yes, and Martha is my client. She is currently awaiting trial for three murders, including Jake's."

Sharon looks horrified, and Hank says, "Your client sounds like a really nice lady. Or should I call her Mom?" This is a bitter guy.

"I believe she will be acquitted of all charges, because she is innocent. What I'm trying to do is learn who might have had reason to kill these people, and why."

"I don't see how I can help you," Hank says. "I don't even know them."

"Your father died a very wealthy man."

Hank laughs a short, derisive laugh. "Good for him."

I continue. "He had a very significant amount of money and extensive land holdings. All of it was left to his wife, Martha, when he died. I believe that wealth is the ultimate reason behind these killings."

Hank shakes his head. "I'm sorry. You come into my home, tell me that my father is dead, and then upset my wife talking about all these murders. What the hell does any of this have to do with me? I haven't seen the man in years, I don't know this Martha, and I don't give a shit that he's dead."

"Hank, don't talk like that," Sharon says, and then turns to me. "I'm sorry, Mr. Carpenter."

"No problem."

I'm torn here; I've been debating whether to tell Hank that there is a chance he could inherit all of the proceeds of Jake's will. I don't have an obligation to, since I'm not his attorney.

Ultimately, I come down on the side of telling him. I want Pups's wishes to be honored and the rescue groups to become the beneficiaries. But the only way that can be honored is if she gets acquitted. And if she does, then she's in control and nothing Hank does can interfere.

Hank's only chance would be if the state took control, and I'd prefer that Hank and Sharon get the money ahead of the state treasury.

I continue. "So I came here to apprise you of the situation, so that if Martha should be convicted, you could attempt to assert your claim. The estate is very substantial." That's a small lie, and I'm withholding the real reason I came here, which was to see if Hank had any involvement or knowledge of a plot to get Pups's money. That does not seem to be the case.

"I don't want anything from him, alive or dead," Hank says.

"Hank, we need to talk about this," Sharon says. "Mr. Carpenter, if we were to look into this, how would we go about it?"

"You'd hire a lawyer who practices estate law."

"How much would that cost?"

"I imagine someone would take the case on a contingency, meaning that he'd only get a fee if you in fact received the inheritance."

I'm not going to get anything more from this conversation, and I know they'll have a lot to discuss with each other, so I say good-bye. I head out to the car, where Tex Miller is waiting for me.

We fly back in the morning, and it's while we're on the first leg that I look out the window at the endless stretches of basically unpopulated land.

It causes me to take out the map of Jake Boyer's land holdings that Walter Tillman sent me. I haven't yet looked at it, but I'm wondering if any of it is near Deadwood.

It's not. The closest is a huge piece of land that, while in South Dakota, is far to the east, north of Chamberlain. It's at least 250 miles from Deadwood. I spend some time trying to find any significance in this, until I fall asleep.

We land at O'Hare to make our connection, and I lose another eight pounds running to the new gate. Overall, I've made no progress on the case, but at least Willie and I got to spend a couple of romantic days together in Deadwood.

I t wasn't the call that unnerved the state senator, Jason Ridgeway, so much.

Since that horrible day in Vegas, he knew the call was coming, even as he dreaded it.

It was the way it happened. They reached him at home
rather than the office. That in itself was enough of an invasion, but even more intrusive was that his wife, Debra,
answered the phone. She came into his office, handed it to
him, and simply said, "It's a Mr. Caffey."

The moment was surreal. He instantly realized that they
had complete control of him. He had known that before, but
somehow this drove the point home in a way that was beyond chilling.

"Hello, Senator, nice to talk to you again. I enjoyed our
meeting in Las Vegas."

"What do you want?"

"Your wife sounds very nice."

"Leave her out of this."

"As long as you do what you're told, Senator. As long as you do what you're told."

"What do you want?"

"You'll receive a package with instructions tomorrow. It will arrive by UPS at your home. Follow the instructions exactly, and you can finally put this whole sordid episode behind you."

Ridgeway started to say that he needed some kind of assurance that whatever it was would be one time only, as they had promised.

But Caffey had already hung up the phone.

**I** finally get home at ten PM, and for a moment I think I'm in the wrong house.

There are Christmas lights everywhere . . . on the tree, along railings, wrapped around table legs, even on the refrigerator. It's blinding and makes Deadwood seem understated.

"We may have overdone it," Laurie tells me, smiling as she comes downstairs to greet me.

"You think?" I ask.

"We had all these extra lights, and Ricky was having such a good time. And then, of course, we bought some more lights. I think Tara and Sebastian might have been a little freaked out at first, but they seem to have adjusted."

"I'm afraid to look in the bathroom," I say.

"No, I drew the line there."

"Good."

She asks me how the trip went, and I tell her there was no significant progress in terms of the case. "Can I tell you about it in the morning?" I ask. "I'm really tired."

"Of course. And call Sam in the morning; he says he has something for you."

"Something good?"

"Sounds like it." She smiles. "I didn't press him, because I know he likes to curry favor directly with the boss."

"How come you never try to curry favor with the boss?"

She smiles again. "I'm too intimidated."

I take Tara and Sebastian for their nightly walk. It's something I like to do at the end of every day, no matter how tired I am, no matter what time it is. But tonight I cut it down to fifteen minutes. By the time we get back, I want nothing more than to collapse into bed and go to sleep. I don't say this lightly, but even if Laurie was in the mood to make love, I'm actually sure that I'd turn her down.

When I get into bed, Laurie is already there, and very much in the mood to make love.

It turns out that I was wrong, and I don't turn her down.

Live and learn.

Tara, Sebastian, and I walk Ricky to school in the morning, and when I get home I call Sam. "I hear you got something, Sam. You know you could tell anything to Laurie; she's part of the team."

"I just figured this was on a need-to-know basis."

Sam thinks he's a CIA operative. "Laurie has top-secret clearance. What have you got for me?"

"I've been checking into Hennessey's phone calls. "There are three that are interesting, all to the same number."

"Tell me about it."

"It's a guy named Frankie Calderone; you probably never heard of him."

"I haven't. Who is he?"

"He's a small-time hood. He's done some time for breaking and entering and had a couple of assault charges dismissed."

I'm not fully understanding why Sam thought this was so significant. It's interesting, but the fact is that Hennessey was not a Boy Scout, and some of his friends could easily have quit the troop as well.

"What's the connection to the case?"

"They spoke the day before the first money was wired. The next time they spoke was twenty minutes after the first wire. Twenty minutes. Third time was twenty minutes after the second wire. And those were the only times they talked. I went back two months."

"Do you know where he is?"

"No idea. I tried tapping into the phone company to get the GPS on his phone, but it's been turned off. Maybe he got rid of it, but I can't find a record of him getting a new number."

"Thanks, Sam, this is very helpful."

As leads go, this is just decent, but compared to what else we have going, it's red hot. I certainly want to find Calderone and talk to him, though I realize he could have a perfectly good explanation for those three phone calls. Maybe they were double dating to the prom that weekend and were working out who would drive and who would buy the corsages.

I could put Marcus on the case, but using just one person could take a while. So I come up with what I think is a better idea.

I take out the private phone number that Big Tiny Parker gave me at the diner, when he offered his help in finding his brother's killer. He said that he had an army of people on the street, privy to all kinds of information.

"Who's talking?" is how he answers the phone.

"Andy Carpenter. You offered to help, and I need some."

"I'm listening."

"There's a guy named Frankie Calderone. All I know about him is that he's a small-time crook and has done some time. I need to talk to him."

"I don't know him," Big Tiny says.

"The question is, Can you find him?"

"If he's still living, and he's around here, I can find him." Then he adds, pointedly, "If I want to. He hit my brother?"

"No," I say quickly. The truth is, I have no idea if Calderone had anything to do with any of the killings, but I don't want Big Tiny to think he did. I want to talk to Calderone, not bury him.

But I also want Big Tiny motivated, so I add, "But he might have some information that could point me in the right direction. The key thing is, if you find him, call me. I'll know what to ask him."

"Stay by the phone," he says.

"It doesn't help us if he gets killed, you understand?"

"Stay by the phone," he says.

**M**y holiday cynicism does not extend to Christmas morning.

I'm a big fan of the whole finding-presents-under-the-tree / drinking-hot-chocolate thing. I don't even mind Christmas music; "Silver Bells" is my particular favorite. And Laurie knows and respects my feelings about Big Crosby, so his fake white Christmas memories are banned from the house.

I'm feeling guilty, of course, since that is my natural state. This time, it's brought on by my being basically a nonparticipant in the present shopping, at least for Ricky. But Laurie has taken up the slack admirably, and Ricky is thrilled with what he's gotten . . . a new baseball glove and a train set. We've also made a donation in his name to the World Wildlife Fund, and every month they'll send him information about an exotic animal he's helped to save.

I bought Laurie a handbag that she took great pains to admire in front of me when we were in the mall one day. Ricky and I also gave her a family cruise to the Caribbean.

Laurie got me two tickets to the Mets home opener and

promised Ricky that if it's a daytime game during the week, he'll be allowed to miss that afternoon of school and go. I think that's the gift he likes the best.

The other gift I got, from the state of New Jersey, is the fact that the holiday keeps the courthouse closed for two weeks, preventing our trial from starting.

We're not nearly ready and not exactly getting closer. It's been four days since I called Big Tiny and gave him the task of finding Calderone, and I haven't heard a word. One more day, and I'm going to let Marcus take a shot at it.

Christmas dinner is terrific; Laurie really nails it. She loves to cook, and her philosophy is that, as a holiday treat, everyone should get exactly what they want. So I have her meatloaf, Rick has fried chicken, and Laurie has grilled salmon and kale.

I've got to tell you, I don't trust kale. Where's it been all these years? How come all of a sudden it appears and is everywhere? Anybody know a kale farmer? Why am I the only one who is worried about a weird plant that all of a sudden shows up? Has no one seen *Invasion of the Body Snatchers*? Or *Little Shop of Horrors*?

Ricky and I both choose banana cream pie for dessert, and we're just finishing up when Big Tiny Parker calls. "I got your boy," he says.

I don't like the sound of that. "You haven't hurt him, have you?"

"Not yet."

"Don't," I say. "He's not the one you want. Where are you?"

"You know Totowa Oval?"

"Yes." Totowa Oval is a park with a baseball field in the Totowa section of Paterson. I had some of my worst baseball performances there as a kid, but it had nothing to do with the field itself. I had terrible baseball performances everywhere I played.

"We'll be by the backstop."

"Give me an hour," I say.

"We'll be here. Don't bring Mr. Marcus."

"OK."

I get off the phone and tell Laurie what's going on.

"Apparently Big Tiny works on holidays, even Christmas Day," she says.

I nod. "Very admirable." Then, "You know I need to go, right? Among other things, I have to make sure they don't kill Calderone."

"Of course," she says.

"Big Tiny told me not to bring Marcus."

She nods. "I'll call Marcus."

Marcus is here in twenty minutes, and it takes another twenty-five to get to Totowa Oval. Once inside the park, it's very dark. When the baseball field comes into sight, I see no sign of anyone.

That changes when a car's lights go on, shining onto the baseball backstop from a distance of maybe ten feet. I can see the shape of four people, three standing and one sitting on the ground, backed up against the backstop. It's not hard to tell from the shape that one of those standing is Big Tiny.

We pull up fairly close to the group and get out. Big Tiny sees Marcus and says, "I told you not to bring him."

"I didn't want to hurt his feelings," I say, walking toward Calderone. He's sitting on the ground, hands tied in front of him, looking scared but unharmed. I don't recognize Big Tiny's two colleagues, and I resist the temptation to ask about the health of the three that Marcus dealt with at the bar.

I lean down to talk to Calderone. "Mr. Calderone, my name is Andy Carpenter. I'm an attorney. I'm sorry to say that I'm the reason you're in this predicament, but it's important that you realize I am also your only chance to get out of it. Do you understand?"

He nods. "Yeah."

"I just have a couple of questions, and if you answer them correctly, which means honestly, then you can go. First one is, tell me about your contact with Randy Hennessey."

"I don't know him."

I shake my head. "Boy, this is off to a bad start. Let's try it again. I know you know him. I know you've talked to him a bunch of times on the phone, so why were you talking to him?"

"I'm telling you, I don't know him."

"OK," I say, standing up. I turn to Big Tiny. "He's no help to me; do whatever you want with him."

He smiles. "Outstanding. You want any souvenirs? Maybe a finger or an arm?"

This seems to motivate Calderone, who says, "I talked to him."

"I told you, I already know that. What did you talk about?"

Calderone hesitates, then looks around at his captors and seems to decide that this is what it is, and he's not going to be able to fool anyone. "I told him to complain about that woman's dogs and that he'd get paid a lot of money for doing it. Then I talked to him a couple of more times about the money."

"Why did you do that? Was it your money?"

"No, man, I don't have that kind of money. He got twenty-five grand."

"So who told you to do it? Who put up the money?"

"Come on, you saw what happened to Hennessey. I've been hiding out, and——"

I interrupt. "Who was it?"

Another hesitation. "His name is Barnett. He's a real estate guy or something."

I don't need Calderone's explanation of who Barnett is; I've already talked to him. He was with Jake Boyer in front of the restaurant when he and Little Tiny were killed.

"What else do you know about Barnett?"

"Not much, I swear. I did some carpentry work at his house a couple of times. But he paid me ten grand to talk to the guy. What was I going to say, no?"

I throw some more questions at Calderone until I'm finally convinced that he's said all that he knows. I finally say, "OK, get up. You can come with us." I've got a feeling that Calderone didn't drive here in his own car; more likely, he was on the floor of Tiny's.

"He ain't goin' nowhere," Big Tiny says, and I can see Calderone react in fear. He's afraid of Big Tiny, which makes perfect sense.

"Actually, Marcus and I think that he is," I say. But even

with Marcus here, I don't want to start trouble, so I add, "You want to find your brother's killer, right? So do I; let me do it my way. This guy had nothing to do with it, but he might be valuable later on. Trust me on this."

I don't know if it's my persuasiveness or Marcus standing there looking like Marcus, but Big Tiny says, "OK, you can get out of here."

We start to walk away, and Calderone says to me, "Thanks, man."

"You'll get a chance to pay me back, if I call on you to testify."

"I don't want to do that," he says.

I shrug. "It's me or Big Tiny . . . your choice."

He looks back at Big Tiny and his crew and says, "OK, I'm with you."

I turn back to Big Tiny, talking softly so that Calderone can't hear me. Big Tiny has to lean down to hear me; otherwise, I'd be whispering into his navel. "I may need him again. Will you be able to find him?"

"That ain't no problem."

**C**affey caught a break.

There was no way he could follow Carpenter into Totowa Oval without being spotted. So, instead, he waited outside and picked up the trail again when Carpenter came out.

The break came when there was a third passenger in the car who wasn't with Carpenter and the guy Caffey assumed was his bodyguard when they went in.

Carpenter dropped the guy off at his car, parked on a side street in downtown Paterson. Caffey decided that it made more sense to follow him than Carpenter, who was probably just headed home. So he did, following him to a dive motel in Englewood.

Fifty bucks to the jerk kid at the front desk got him the man's name, Frank Calderone. The name meant nothing to Caffey, since he was not involved in the recruitment of Randy Hennessey.

But it was certainly something that needed to be reported in, so Caffey called one of his employers and described the events of the evening. He could not relate any conversations that took place inside the park, of course, but he didn't have to.

The employer, David Barnett, knew that if Calderone had been under any stress, and he almost certainly had, then he would give up Barnett's name.

It was information that Barnett would keep to himself, especially since the situation could be managed. The negative was that Carpenter now knew for certain that Barnett was involved, and it would guide him in his investigation.

But this development in and of itself did not involve legal jeopardy for Barnett; it was more in the area of an annoyance. And if the situation deteriorated, then Calderone or Carpenter could be eliminated.

Or both.

**A**ll doubt has been removed.

    If there was any question that Pups is innocent or that the Hennessey killing is part of a larger conspiracy, it no longer exists. I now know that eighteen months ago David Barnett took Jake Boyer to dinner and to his execution.

Of course, even though I am totally convinced, I am very unlikely to be chosen as a member of the jury. And there is very little here, even if it were admissible, that would convince the twelve people we will impanel.

Legally, what I have is of very little value. There's no evidence tying Barnett to Jake's murder, and the only thing connecting him to Hennessey is Calderone's word.

Tressel would salivate at the opportunity to cross-examine Calderone. He's a convicted felon who cannot even explain why Barnett chose him to deal with Hennessey. They come from different worlds, and the connection would be hard to believe. Add to that the fact that Calderone has the personal charm and credibility of a delinquent weasel, and he'd get me nowhere if I put him on the stand.

For the moment, I can take comfort in the fact that Barnett does not know that I'm on to him. If Calderone was telling the truth about having only necessary, isolated contact with Barnett, then their direct relationship ended a while ago.

Calderone is scared; by his own admission, he's been hiding out. The idea that he would volunteer to Barnett, a man he believes engineered Hennessey's murder, the fact that he gave me Barnett's name, defies common sense. Barnett may eventually find out that I know of his role in this, but it seems highly doubtful that he knows it yet.

So for the moment it is information that I have in my pocket, and the major positive is that it helps provide a road map for my investigation.

Barnett is something of a wheeler-dealer in real estate, that much I know to be true. He told me that on the night of the murder, he had been at the restaurant conveying an offer to purchase land to Jake Boyer. There is a chance that is true as well. In fact, maybe Barnett gave some kind of sign after dinner to signal whether the shooting was on or off, depending on Jake's response to the offer. Accepting the offer might well have saved his life.

Walter Tillman calls to ask me if I located Jake Boyer's son.

"I did. He's married and dealing blackjack at Cadillac Jack's Gaming Resort in Deadwood, South Dakota."

"Sounds like a classy establishment," he says.

"They do make a good steak."

"You actually went out there?" he says, the amusement and surprise evident in his voice.

"I did. I had a nice talk with Hank. He is not mourning his father's death."

"I'm not surprised. Did you happen to tell him about his possible claim to the will, in the unlikely event that Pups is convicted?"

"I did. He was unimpressed and uninterested, but his wife may convince him otherwise."

"Well, I'm glad you did. I haven't nailed this down, but I think informing him is an ethical obligation of mine, which you have just fulfilled. Will you sign a document saying that you informed him?"

"Sure," I say.

"Andy, you do nice work; I may make you my permanent emissary to obscure Western places. Meanwhile, I'll prepare the document and e-mail it over. Did you get the check for your fee?"

"I did, thanks." It had come while I was in South Dakota. Pups is paid in full.

I head down to the jail to speak to Pups. I do this despite knowing that she will yell at me for not having dog photos to bring with me. I am a walking profile in courage.

Pups is coughing a little more each time I see her, but she tells me that they're experimenting with medications to help that symptom.

The main difference between visiting her and visiting other clients in similar situations is that she never asks me about developments in her case. I'm not sure what that's about, though of course I'd like to think she trusts me. But usually clients bombard me with questions. Not Pups.

"Merry Christmas," I say, when she's brought in.

"Tell me about it."

" 'Twas the night before Christmas, and all through the house, not a creature was—"

"Can it," she says, so I do. "You got pictures?"

"No, but Willie has some that I'll bring next time. All the puppies were adopted, and the mother is going to a home tomorrow."

"And Puddles?"

"Doing great. I told the little girl about the reverse pet; she already knew all about it and has been executing it flawlessly."

"Good."

"Let me ask you a question. Walter Tillman told me that you have turned down a number of offers to sell some of your land."

"Jake's land," is how she corrects me. "What's your question?"

I nod. "Jake's land. Did you actually get and turn down offers?"

"Yeah. Jake never wanted to sell, so I didn't either. Why?"

"When you got the offers, were they submitted in writing?" I ask.

"I think so."

"Did you keep those documents?"

She thinks for a moment. "I'm sure I would have. Everything related to the land I put in Jake's file."

"Would Jake have kept copies of the offers that came to him?"

"Definitely. He was a stickler for having things in writing, and he never threw anything away. If he got offers, they're in that file."

"I need to see that file," I say. "Where is it?"

"In my basement. But if you go down there, bring a flashlight. It's dark and very dusty."

Hmmm. Searching through the old files of a deceased man in a dingy, dark basement . . . if ever there was a job that fit Hike's personality, this was it.

So I call Hike and give him the assignment, and he asks, "Are there rats down there?"

"I don't think so, Hike, but I will admit that I've never been in that particular basement. Pups didn't mention anything about rats."

"You ever see a man die from rat bites?" he asks.

"I don't believe I have."

"I can send you a link to a video of it. It's not pretty."

"That's OK, I'd rather not see it," I say. "This being Christmas and all."

"OK, but one rat and I'm out of there."

"Fair enough."

**T**he job takes Hike the better part of three days.

As he describes it, the basement is a jungle of paper and all kinds of other stuff; apparently, Jake and Pups had never thrown anything away. Jake's papers were in various places in the basement, and, even once Hike found them, deciphering his filing system was a task comparable to breaking the Nazi codes in World War II.

Hike sometimes has a tendency to negatively embellish.

He's put together all the relevant documents, and we're meeting in my office with Sam Willis. I'm going to give them a job to do together, a fact that will please neither. They get along OK, except for the fact that Sam considers Hike a downbeat creep, and Hike considers Sam a psycho pain in the ass.

Hike brings four thick folders full of papers to our meeting. "It's every scrap having to do with the land that he bought over the years," Hike says. "Tax documents, local easements, everything. As far as I can tell, it's all still part of the estate, although they've had many offers to buy pieces of it."

"Are there written offer sheets?"

He nods. "Definitely. Of course, there could be some missing; I'd have no way of knowing that. But there are a lot of them, some to him and some to our client after he died. None were accepted."

"OK, here's what I need you to do," I say. "You'll be working together." I don't hear any moans, so I continue. "I want these holdings dissected to find out if any of these pieces have hidden value. Has gold been discovered all around it? Does somebody want to build a casino on it? I can't tell you exactly what you're looking for, but you'll know it if you find it."

Sam nods. "Got it."

"Good, because most of the burden will fall on you. You guys can't travel to all these places, so the great majority of the work, if not all, will have to be done online. If there are any legal filings or issues involved, Hike can analyze it for meaning. But Hike will be with me in court, so his time will be limited."

I continue. "Look at all of it, but pay special attention to any pieces of land on which Jake or Pups got multiple offers, and very special attention to any offers that came through David Barnett. Hike, you can separate it all out, to make Sam's job easier. I also want to get as much information as I can about each of the parties making these offers."

"This is a big job," Sam says.

"I know. Is your team available?"

"I don't see why not. Hanukah's over." Sam taught a computer class for seniors at the YMHA, and four of his top students were Hilda and Eli Mandlebaum, Morris Fishman, and Leon Goldberg. Each of them has been on social security almost since FDR invented it, but they are tireless workers on the computer. They've helped out on a few cases in the past and have been invaluable. Plus, Hilda makes chicken soup to die for.

"Great. Sam, I also need you to find out everything you can about David Barnett. Business, personal life—everything."

"I'm on it. You want me to put a tail on him?"

"A tail?"

"You know, a stakeout. I can watch him and work on the computer at the same time. I have wireless in my car."

"No stakeout necessary this time, Sam. No shooting either."

He nods. "OK, but the option is available if you need it."

"Thanks. OK, guys, we need this yesterday."

I spend the next few days in intense pretrial preparation. Mercifully, Laurie has the same view of New Year's Eve parties as I do, so we stay home and watch the ball drop on TV. Ricky wants us to wake him to see it, so we do that.

We wake him at ten to midnight, and he comes into the den to watch it with us. He's back asleep at five of, but we wake him again in three minutes. It's Laurie, Ricky, me, Tara and Sebastian, all on or around the couch, watching a year end and a new one begin.

There's a scene in a very underrated eighties comedy called

*About Last Night.* A twentyish Demi Moore has cooked Thanksgiving dinner, and afterward she is scrubbing a pot in the kitchen sink. It's hard work, and she holds the dirty pot up and says to Elizabeth Perkins, "It's official. I've become my mother."

Sitting here on the couch with my entire family, I don't know when all this happened. Yesterday I was single and on my own, and today I have a wife, child, and two dogs.

It's official, I have become my father.

And I wouldn't have it any other way.

I t was almost the perfect crime," Tressel says. "In fact, for two years, it was just that."

He shakes his head, as if amazed by the brilliance of the plot. "Jake Boyer comes out of a restaurant and gets gunned down. Anybody who's ever watched *Law and Order* knows that among the first people that the police look at and try to eliminate as a suspect is the spouse. It's police work 101."

The jurors that we impaneled, five men and seven women, are hanging on every word. Some are even nodding, alerting Tressel to the fact that they have indeed watched *Law and Order.* Being a juror is a new experience for them, and they're eager to get into it. Later on, it will be hard to keep them awake.

"And what was the awful brilliance behind it? It was the addition of a second victim, a known gang member, who himself lived in a world of violence. It had the effect of making the real target seem like an innocent bystander, and the bystander seem like the real target. So the police went in that direction, and who can blame them?

"But it turns out that the spouse, Martha Boyer," he says as he points to Pups, "was the killer all along. And how do we know that? Because she killed again. Randall Hennessey annoyed her. He had the temerity to get her angry, so she killed him. With the same gun. Let me repeat that. Three people, a year and a half apart, were killed with the same gun.

"And where was this triple-murder weapon found? In Martha Boyer's basement, no more than two hours after Randall Hennessey died.

"Martha Boyer had killed before, at least twice that we know of. Maybe she liked it; maybe she just thought she could get away with it again. I can't know for sure what went through her mind, but she obviously believed that it was a viable option again.

"There are a number of factors that make this case different from most others. It may come up during the course of the trial, or it may not. But a number of you, during jury selection, indicated that you knew about it, so we might as well get it on the table.

"Doctors have apparently told the defendant, Martha Boyer, that she has a terminal illness. I can't myself confirm the accuracy of that diagnosis, and I won't try. But the point, the key point, is that it should have no effect on what you do here.

"The tendency of good people like yourselves might be to feel sorry for her, and that sympathy might cloud your judgment and affect your decision. Let me state this as clearly as I can: you cannot let that happen.

"Martha Boyer does not deserve your sympathy or your compassion. She had no compassion for Jake Boyer or Raymond Parker or Randall Hennessey. What she did to them was terminal and brutal and undeserved. And their memories demand justice, the kind of justice that only you can provide. Her health is not your concern; your concern should be to declare, on behalf of the state of New Jersey and Passaic County, that we will not tolerate murder, and we will punish those who commit it.

"We will prove to you, beyond a reasonable doubt, beyond a shadow of a doubt, that Martha Boyer killed these three people. That is my solemn duty and that of my colleagues. And then you have a solemn duty to perform, and I know you will do so with intelligence and impartiality. Thank you for listening, and thank you for your service."

As Tressel talks, I can see Pups getting angry. I have two worries. One, that the jury will see the same thing and decide she has a temper. And, two, that she will jump up and grab Tressel by the throat. That would be what we lawyers call prejudicial.

Hopefully, my opening statement will calm her somewhat.

"Ladies and gentlemen, I'm going to do a role reversal here, at least up to a point. Traditionally, the prosecutor will get up and extol the police for having done a wonderful job in finding the guilty party, using brilliant detecting techniques to bring him or her to justice. That is because the prosecutor and police are always on the same side, and their shared goal is to convict the accused.

"The defense, which in this case is me, usually argues the

opposite. We point to errors that the police made, crucial errors that ultimately led them to accuse the wrong person while the actual guilty party goes free.

"But this time it's different: the process is turned on its head, and I'm going to be honest with you about it. Mr. Tressel is telling you that in the investigation of the murders of Jake Boyer and Raymond Parker, the police were hapless blunderers. They completely missed the real killer, he says, even though he admits that the spouse is the first person they always look to.

"He will have you believe that they just missed it entirely; in fact, they couldn't even get the target right, never mind the killer. They messed up badly, he said, but great news: this time, the same dopes got it right."

I shake my head in wonder at the ridiculousness of it all.

"And now I'm on the other side. And forgive me if I stumble a bit, because I'm not used to praising police work." I smile, and the jury smiles with me.

"But you know what? There's one thing the police got right eighteen months ago. They nailed it. They investigated Martha Boyer thoroughly, ticked off every box, and they came up with nothing. And you know why? It's because there was nothing to be found.

"The police were right back then, after as intensive an investigation as this city has ever seen. They were right in saying that Martha Boyer was innocent, and no amount of revisionist history can change that.

"I was not going to bring up Martha Boyer's terrible illness; I felt she deserved more privacy than that. But Mr. Tressel felt otherwise, so I now have to discuss it. All I want to say is that there are better ways to spend your last days than listening to the state of New Jersey say you are a murderer and that among the people you murdered was the man you loved more than anyone in the world.

"But Martha Boyer wants her own justice, and she wants her reputation, and she wants to lay claim to her own memory. That is why she did not plead guilty in order to avoid the emotional horror of this trial. She has dedicated her life to helping the helpless, in her case unwanted young animals, and she wants to be remembered for that. Not for horrible crimes that she did not commit.

"Thank you."

I'm feeling pretty good about my statement as I return to the defense table, and then Judge Chambers has to go and kill the mood with six frightening and depressing words.

"Mr. Tressel, call your first witness."

**D**etective Curtis Hayslett was in charge of the double-murder investigation at the Bonfire Restaurant.

I'm sure Tressel would rather focus on the Hennessey murder, but he can't look like he's hiding from the restaurant killings, so he wants to get it out and behind him as soon as he can. It's not terrible ground for him, but the rest of his case is stronger.

He starts out by having Hayslett literally set the scene, describing what he saw when he pulled up to the restaurant that night. Hayslett says that there were two dead males on the street and a number of witnesses, including a man who had just had dinner with one of the deceased.

"That was David Barnett?" Tressel asks.

"Yes, he had dinner with Mr. Boyer. He was with him when he died but was fortunately unhit by the gunfire."

"Did you recognize either of the victims before you were told who they were?"

"Yes, I knew Mr. Parker by reputation because of his alleged gang involvement."

"Was it your initial assumption that he was the target of the shooting?"

Hayslett shakes his head; he's not going to go down without a fight. "I don't make initial assumptions; I follow the facts."

"But independent of these events. If someone had told you before they happened that Mr. Parker might be involved in a shooting, you would not have been shocked?"

"I think that's fair to say."

"You ultimately settled on Mr. Parker as the likely target, did you not?"

"Ultimately."

"Are you aware that the police commissioner, Mr. Wentz, publicly referred to this as a gang shooting three days after it took place?"

"I don't recall that. But I can tell you that I would not have been ready to say that then. I was just beginning my investigation. Nor did the commissioner ever discuss the case with me or direct me to follow a certain theory."

Hayslett is not showing political courage by disagreeing with the commissioner, since he was replaced in the job a year ago when a new administration came in.

Tressel gets him to admit that it wasn't too long before the primary focus was on Parker as the target, but it's a grudging admission. Hayslett is not going to let himself be seen as the cop who blew it. Blowing it would mean his incompetence kept Pups out of jail, which led to Hennessey's death.

It's a very tough position for him to be in, because while he doesn't want to admit he screwed up back then, he certainly doesn't want to jeopardize the current prosecution.

My first question on cross-examination is, "Looking back on those two murders, do you think you rushed to judgment?"

He shakes his head. "I do not."

"Was Mr. Tressel right in his opening statement when he said that the spouse is the first person the police look at? He said that's how they do it on *Law and Order*." The jury and gallery laugh at my making fun of Tressel, though his face remains impassive.

"We certainly carefully check into the motivations of those who knew and were close to the victim, and that obviously includes the spouse."

"So that's a yes?" I ask.

"It's a qualified yes."

"Did Ms. Boyer have what is commonly referred to as an alibi?"

He nods. "She did. She said that she was playing bridge with friends at the time of the shooting."

"And you confirmed that with her bridge partners?"

"Of course. They all supported her story."

"So you saw no way she could have been the actual shooter?"

"That's correct," he says.

"Has your view on that changed over time, or do you feel the same way today?"

"I feel the same way today. She could not have personally been there."

"What about other evidence that might have pointed toward her guilt? Any signs of marital discord? Arguments over money? Either of them having an affair? Anything at all?"

Tressel objects that I need to ask one question at a time, and Chambers sustains, so I ask it in a more concise fashion, and Hayslett admits that there was no such evidence.

"So even in light of recent events, is it fair to say that you don't know how Ms. Boyer might have done it, or why?"

"That's fair. But that doesn't mean she didn't do it."

"Thanks for sharing that, Detective. Did you also investigate Mr. Boyer, independent of his wife's possible involvement? Did you consider that he could have been the target, but the killer could have been someone else?"

"I considered everything."

"Including the possibility that while Mr. Boyer might have been the target, it could have been business-related?

He nods. "Yes."

"What business was Mr. Boyer in?"

"I don't remember."

"Does that mean you didn't focus on that aspect?"

"It doesn't mean that at all," he says.

"It just means you don't remember," I say, more as a hopefully revealing commentary than a question. My goal here is to open up the possibility that the killing was related to Jake Boyer's business without presenting evidence to that effect.

"Yes," he says.

"Detective, in your entire investigation, other than the fact that Mr. Parker had gang connections, did you find any other evidence which confirmed that he was the target that night?"

"No."

I have to be careful here, because Tressel is likely unaware that I am also going to contend that Jake Boyer was the target, though of course for different reasons, and by a different killer than he will accuse. So I can't push it further right now.

"Thank you, Detective. No further questions."

I am in a ridiculous, frustrating position.

I know that Pups is innocent, and it's not simply because of my basic trust in her. The connection, through Calderone, between Barnett, who was there the night Jake Boyer was murdered, and Hennessey, a subsequent victim himself, convinces me beyond a reasonable doubt.

But the jury? Since we cannot get the Barnett-Hennessey connection before them in a way that is particularly credible, the jury will have enough doubt of my theory to overflow the jury box.

Our contention will appear ludicrous on its face. We are saying that someone killed Jake Boyer, then waited almost two years to frame Pups for a subsequent murder. If that's the case, then why didn't they just frame Pups for Jake's murder in the first place and cut out the middle victim?

And why wait until Pups is dying, which is not exactly a secret, to frame her? Why would anybody go to the trouble and risk of committing a murder to incarcerate her, only to have her die in jail in a few months?

It doesn't even make sense to me, and I know it's true.

During the afternoon court break, I get a message from Sam to come to his office later so he and Hike can update me on their progress going through Jake's land-related papers. He doesn't say they've found anything particularly exciting, which is a shame, because our case could use a truckload of exciting.

Tressel's next witness is Walter Tillman. I lodge an objection because, as their attorney, anything Jake and Pups may have said to him is privileged. That's true even after the death of a client.

Chambers correctly overrules my objection once Tressel says that Tillman is merely there to discuss the contents of Jake's will. That will, once admitted to probate, became part of the public record, so Tillman would not be breaking privilege by describing it.

Tillman is certainly friendly toward Pups, but he's still Tressel's best choice to accomplish this task, because he's there merely to state the facts. He's ideal to do that, since he wrote the will in the first place.

As Tillman takes the stand, he gives me a small smile and shrug, as if to say he wishes he didn't have to be here. What he doesn't realize is that I'm glad he is.

Once Tressel gets Tillman to confirm his legal relationship to both Boyers, he asks him if he prepared Jake Boyer's will.

"I did," Tillman says.

"Who was the beneficiary of that will?"

"His wife, Martha Boyer."

"The sole beneficiary?"

"Yes."

"And when Mr. Boyer was murdered, did she receive the contents of the estate as directed in the document?"

"She did."

"In general terms, what was in the estate?" Tressel asks.

"Close to fifteen million dollars in investments and liquid assets and a great deal of real estate scattered around the country."

"What kind of real estate?"

"A small amount of commercial property, but mostly large parcels of unused land."

"Can you estimate the value of that property?"

"Not accurately, but quite substantial," Tillman says.

"Seven figures?" Tressel prods.

"No, I'm quite certain it's eight figures."

Tillman was called simply to provide a financial motive for Pups to have murdered Jake, and he's done that, so Tressel turns him over to me.

I stand up as Hike hands me a piece of paper. "Your Honor, with the permission of the court, I would like to present this document to Mr. Tillman. It is a waiver of privilege for all communications between Martha Boyer and Mr. Tillman, regarding all matters."

Judge Chambers looks at it and allows it, and I give it to Tillman. "Mr. Tillman, you are now free to relate any conversation and business you've had with your client, Martha Boyer. She specifically requests that you not respect the privilege."

He nods. "I understand."

"Mr. Tillman, you've testified that you prepared and executed Jake Boyer's will, which left his entire estate to his wife, Martha. He did so freely?"

"Of course."

"You were his friend as well?"

"Definitely. I considered Jake a close friend."

"In your capacity as friend, would you say that the Boyers had a good marriage?"

"Yes."

"No talk of splitting up, no violence, no unusual anger?"

"I never saw anything like that, and Jake never even hinted at anything like that."

"And he was perfectly happy to leave everything to Martha," I point out.

He nods. "He was."

"You testified about the large amount of money and real estate inherited by Martha Boyer. You've now prepared her will; how much of that is left?"

"All of it."

I shake my head as if he didn't understand. "No, I mean how much has she burned through in a wild spending spree?"

He smiles. "None of it. She lives a very frugal life. Basically, the only substantial money she spends is for taking care of the dogs and medical bills for herself."

"So her financial life has been the same before and after her husband's death?"

"Very much so, yes."

Just in case the jury hasn't gotten the point, I say, "So just to be clear: you see no way she benefited financially from her husband's death?"

"Correct."

"And who is the beneficiary of Martha Boyer's will?"

"A large collection of animal rescue groups."

"Thank you. No further questions."

**H**ike and I get to Sam's office at four thirty. He's there with the computer crew: Hilda, Eli, Morris, and Leon. They would have left already, but they've waited for me so they could say hello. They start their day by six AM, so by this time they're fading fast.

They're an amazing group, as enthusiastic as any people I have ever met. Even Hike seems to perk up when they're around. They're in their eighties; I hope I'm that active when I'm in my fifties.

Hilda tells me that I'm looking thin, which would tend to indicate that, while her mind and body are healthy and vibrant, her eyes are deteriorating. She promises to make and bring rugelach, a Jewish pastry, with her tomorrow. I have had Hilda's rugelach, and if I were about to be executed, it would be my choice for last meal.

When they leave, we sit at Sam's small conference table so they can take me through what they've learned. Sam acts as the spokesman, simply because he's done much more work on this than Hike has, since Hike's been in court with me. Hike is probably going to hear much of this for the first time.

"So, to start, I've prepared a map which shows the land holdings that now belong to our client," Sam says. He hands out sheets with a color map of the United States, clearly marked to show where the land is. Most of it is in the middle of the country, but there are pieces as far west as Arizona, and as far east as North Carolina.

"As you can see," he continues, "it's very spread out, but the largest parcels, in terms of acreage, are in South Dakota and Iowa. This piece in South Dakota is almost ten thousand acres, and the one in Iowa is maybe 30 percent smaller than that. The land is essentially uninhabited, though I'd have to drive it to know that for sure. There could be squatters on it."

He goes on. "There are records of twenty-eight concrete offers, plus fifteen of what I would call interested feelers, on the properties. Of these, seven were for the South Dakota land, and four for the Iowa land. By far, the most money was offered for these parcels. The highest offer in South Dakota was four and a half million dollars, and in Iowa the top offer was three million four.

"David Barnett represented the potential buyers in three of the South Dakota offers and two of the Iowa offers."

"On whose behalf was he making the offers?" I ask.

"That's where it gets interesting. The offers were made by an outfit that calls itself Imperial Real Estate Partners. It's incorporated in the Cayman Islands."

"So you can't tell who the main players are," I say.

He nods. "Right. They're shielded down there."

"Do you have any idea why they wanted this land?" I ask.

He shakes his head. "We're not there yet. We're just start-ing to dig into that now."

"OK. For the time being, limit your focus to the South Dakota and Iowa properties that Barnett conveyed offers on. Is there anything in the papers to indicate that Jake had spe-cific reasons for declining the offers? Might he have been aware of some hidden value?"

"Nothing like that at all, Andy. Obviously, there might have been some verbal communications going on, but there's no evidence that Jake responded at all. He may just have had no interest."

"Thanks, Sam. Great work."

I'm feeling like this is coming into focus more, but I still don't understand the whys behind it all. Even if this land is sitting on a trillion dollars' worth of diamonds, how does kill-ing Jake and framing Pups get the bad guys closer to it?

I guess one possibility would be that if Pups is convicted and loses the inheritance, then New Jersey would sell off the estate for its own treasury. Maybe the killers think they have a way into the Jersey officials that will supervise the land sale and can get it for far less than what they know it to be worth.

It's a possibility, but a very slim one. There is no way they could be close to confident that it could be orchestrated, and all the attention of the killings and the trial has shined a light on Jake's estate that would make a scheme like that even tougher.

There has to be something else going on.

When I get home, Ricky and Laurie are waiting for me. I've promised to help with the only operation that's almost as bad as decorating the Christmas tree, and that is undecorating the tree.

I've been putting it off, but it's turning brown, and Laurie and Ricky have let me know that it's time. Getting the strings of lights off the damn tree would be challenging for a NASA engineer, and it's way beyond my level of competence.

My preference would be to throw the tree out with the lights still on it, then get a new tree next year with new lights. "It would be starting over," I tell Laurie. "Like a rebirth. Very inspiring and meaningful."

That goes over like a string of dead lights, so I suffer through the whole operation. The lights are a pain to remove, but the ornaments . . . my God, the ornaments.

Finally, we're finished, and it's Ricky's bedtime. We've developed a ritual that I really like, in which we do a little football trivia as I'm tucking him in. He's been reading a book for kids about NFL Super Bowls, and his retention of it is amazing.

"Who played in the first Super Bowl?" I ask.

He frowns. "That's easy. Green Bay and Kansas City."

"Who won?"

"Dad, come one. Make them harder. Green Bay."

"Who was the MVP?"

This causes him to think for a moment. "Bart Starr."

I kiss him on the head. "You're too good."

I turn to leave, and he says, "Dad?"

"What is it?"

"Will you take me to a Super Bowl someday?"

"Rick, it will be my pleasure."

**D**avid Barnett is Tressel's next witness. As he takes the stand, I have no idea if he is aware that I know he got Calderone to put Hennessey up to complaining about Pups's dogs. I will operate under the assumption that he does know, because even though I doubt that Calderone would tell him, it's possible that the resourceful Barnett found out another way.

Tressel is calling him because he was a witness to the murders of Jake and Little Tiny. "Were you at the Bonfire Restaurant the night that Jake Boyer and Raymond Parker were shot?" he asks.

"I was. I had dinner with Mr. Boyer."

"Were you friends?"

"I would say that we were business associates, but we had a number of interactions, so I would say we were friendly, if not friends. I certainly liked him."

"You were discussing business that night?"

"Yes, though I can't recall what the particular subject was.

The events after dinner made whatever it was rather unimportant."

"Tell the court what happened when you left the restaurant."

"We had driven to the restaurant together in his car, but when we got there the lot was full, so we parked around the corner. After dinner, we walked to the car, and, when we reached it, there were some young men standing nearby. I believe the house we parked in front of was where at least one of the young men lived."

"Did you recognize any of the young men?"

"No. They were wearing what I felt was gang paraphernalia, with the inscription 'Bloodz' on it." He spells out B-l-o-o-d-z for the benefit of the jury and then grins. "It seemed to me they might be with a gang of some sort, so I was rather anxious to get into the car."

"So you got into the car?"

He nods. "Quickly, which probably saved my life. I heard rapid-fire shots; I used to belong to a gun club, so I immediately recognized what they were. I dived down, but I could see they came from a passing car. I'm afraid I couldn't see the shooter or identify the type of car. When it was over, I looked around and saw Jake and that young man, lying on the ground."

"What did you do next?"

"Nothing. I searched for my phone; in the excitement, I must have dropped it. By the time I found it, the police were on the scene. One of the other bystanders must have called them."

Tressel asks him a few more questions, really just to set the horror of the scene, and then he turns him over to me. "Mr. Barnett," I start, "you testified that you had business with Jake Boyer that night, but you can't recall the exact nature of it?"

"That's right."

"What business are you in?"

"Real estate."

"So it's fair to say that the business would have involved real estate?" I ask.

"Yes."

"Was Jake Boyer in the real estate business?"

"He was mostly retired, but he owned quite a bit of real estate around the country."

"Did you ever try to sell any to him?"

"No, I don't believe so," he says.

"Did you ever try to buy any?"

"Yes."

"Did he ever sell any to you?"

"No, he liked to hold on to what he had. He would say that land wasn't going anywhere, that things disappear, but land doesn't."

"Did you make similar offers to Ms. Boyer?"

"I believe that I did, yes. Not as many."

"Did she accept any?"

"No. Her attitude was the same as her husband's."

I could ask him if he knows Randall Hennessey, in the hopes that I could at least get him on perjury later if he denies it and I could prove otherwise. But doing so would be a red flag to him, and he would know for sure that I'm aware of their contact. So I hold off and let him off the stand, but I tell Judge Chambers to inform him that he is subject to recall in the defense case.

I'm making some progress on cross-examination, but I'm just making pin pricks in Tressel's case. The way things are going, at the end of the day the elephant in the room is going to be the gun in the basement.

The jury knows that the same gun was used in both shootings and that that gun was found in Pups's basement. It remains a devastating piece of evidence. I've got to put on a defense case that not only casts reasonable doubt on Pups's guilt but also points to an alternative guilty party.

I can put Calderone on the stand to testify that Barnett paid him to approach Hennessey, and hopefully he would do so honestly. But he would make a very shaky witness, and Tressel could easily destroy his credibility. I need another way to tie Barnett to Calderone to bolster that credibility.

During a break in the court session, I do something that I should have done before. I call Sam to put him on the Calderone case.

"Sam, I know you and your team are overloaded, but I need you to do a cyberexam on Frankie Calderone. Phone calls in and out around the same dates as his contacts with Hennessey and a full financial as well."

"What is it you're looking for?" he asks.

"I want to connect him to David Barnett. Get me anything I can use."

"Hilda's got some downtime; I'll put her right on it."

"She knows what she's doing?" I ask.

"Andy, Hilda is better at hacking than she is at rugelach."

Luther Crenshaw is a tough cop who has seen it all.

He's got to be nearing retirement age, but when he gets there, he's going to have to be carried off kicking and screaming. Pete once told me that Luther is the single best cop he's ever been around. Coming from him, that was a huge and memorable statement.

I expected Luther to testify a little later in the trial, but Tressel must not be happy with the way things are going, so he's changed the order and brought in his big gun now. The jury will then see everything else in the light of what Luther has to say.

Tressel asks Luther what brought him to the Hennessey murder scene, and he says a 911 call. "Who made that call, if you know?"

Luther nods. "It was the defendant, Martha Boyer."

"What did you do when you arrived on the scene?"

"I had my people secure the area, and I spoke to Ms. Boyer, who was waiting there for me."

"What did she say?"

"That she saw the body of Randall Hennessey in his kitchen, that he appeared to have been wounded badly in his head, and that she believed he was deceased."

"Did she tell you how she happened to be in his kitchen?" Tressel asks.

"She told me that Mr. Hennessey called her."

"What did she say was the purpose of the call?"

"He wanted to give her a gift of some sort," Luther says, with a very slight smile on his face.

"What did you tell her?"

"To wait in a squad car until I came back to her. I then went in to Mr. Hennessey's house and found the body in the kitchen, as she described it."

Tressel then takes Luther through a rather tedious discussion about securing the scene and directing forensics. Finally, he gets back to Martha. "Did you know anything about the relationship between Martha Boyer and Randall Hennessey?"

He nods. "I did; I had seen in the media that she had threatened him. I asked if we could enter and search her house, to negate the necessity of getting a warrant. She agreed."

"And you searched the house?"

He nods. "We did. We found a gun in the basement."

"And were forensics tests done on the gun?" Tressel asks.

I could object to this line of questioning because Luther was not involved in the tests, but I'll deal with it on cross.

"They were. And it came up as a match against the gun that killed Jake Boyer and Tiny Parker a year and a half prior."

"Just to be clear. Forensics conclusively demonstrated that the gun found in Martha Boyer's basement killed Randall Hennessey, Raymond Parker, and Jake Boyer?"

"That is correct," Luther says.

"No further questions."

I start my cross-examination with, "Detective Crenshaw, you talked about the forensics match on the gun. Did you conduct those tests yourself?"

"I did not."

"Were there other tests on the gun that you have information about? Such as fingerprints?"

"The gun was tested for prints, and there were none. It was wiped clean."

"So the way you figure it, Ms. Boyer committed a murder with that gun, wiped it clean of prints, and then ran home to hide it in her own basement?"

"She might have planned to discard the gun later," he says.

"Then why bother wiping it clean to put in her basement?"

"Only she can answer that."

"I think you mean, only the person who put it in her basement can answer that," I say.

Tressel objects that I'm putting words in the witness's mouth, and Chambers sustains the objections, because in fact I'm putting words in the witness's mouth.

"By the way, Detective, you said that Ms. Boyer claimed the victim called her."

He nods. "That's right."

"Did you check the phone records? Was a call made from Mr. Hennessey to Ms. Boyer?"

"The call was made from his house," he carefully says.

I nod as if it's all clear now. "So you think she might have made the call to cover for herself?"

"It's possible."

"Was the call answered?" I ask.

"Yes."

"So you think she made a call, raced home, and answered it herself?" I point to Pups. "This lady did that?"

"The machine could have answered."

"Did you find evidence of that?" I ask.

"No."

"Detective, once you found that the gun was also used in the murders eighteen months ago, did you familiarize yourself with that investigation?"

He nods. "To some degree, yes."

"Are you aware that Detective Hayslett testified earlier in this trial that Ms. Boyer was fully able to account for her time when her husband was murdered and that he was certain she was not on the scene and did not pull the trigger herself?"

"I didn't follow his testimony, but I know that is his view."

"Do you share that view?"

"Based on the available information, yes."

"Yet Ms. Boyer is on trial here in the courtroom for those murders. Is the assumption that she got someone else to do the shooting for her?"

"I would assume so, yes."

"Like a hit man."

He frowns. "When you hire a man to make a hit, that does make him a hit man, yes."

"So please tell the court how you think the gun was handled."

"What do you mean?"

"Well, for example, whose gun is it? Do you think she hired a hit man who said to her, 'This is embarrassing, but can I borrow your gun? I don't have one, and I promise I'll return it after I kill your husband'?"

"I don't know. I . . ."

"Don't hit men generally own their own guns, sort of their tools of the trade? When they set out to make murder their career, isn't that the first thing they get?"

He looks worried, unsure of where to go with this, and the gallery is laughing at him. "I would assume the killer had his own gun."

I nod. "I see; that makes sense. And then after he killed her husband, he gave it to Ms. Boyer as a souvenir to commemorate the occasion? And she kept it in a trophy case, until one day deciding to use it to kill Mr. Hennessey?"

"What's important is that it is the same gun."

"That's what's important to you, Detective, because you're trying to make a case where none exists. What we do here in court is present the facts to the jury, and then they decide what is important."

Tressel objects, but Chambers overrules him.

"Do you have a theory on whose gun this was, the hit man's or Ms. Boyer's. And why, according to you, both of them used the same gun a year and a half apart?"

"I can't be sure what happened, no."

"Detective, since you seem to be up on the forensics

testing that was done on this case, were Martha Boyer's hands and clothes tested for gunpowder residue?"

"They were."

"Was any found?"

"No."

"How do you explain that?"

"She could have washed it off."

"She washed her clothes as well?"

"It's possible."

"Was there any evidence of that? Wet clothes? Clothes in the dryer?"

"No. She could also have disposed of them after the shooting."

"And ran naked back to her house? Did you find discarded clothes when you searched the area?"

"No, but she could have effectively disposed of them."

"So let me see if I can sum up. She shot Mr. Hennessey, called herself from his house and then ran home to take the call, pausing to strip naked and dispose of her clothes somewhere you couldn't find them, wiped the gun clean of prints and hid it in the basement rather than disposing of it with the clothes, washed her hands, got dressed, and then called 911? Is that the official police theory?"

Tressel objects, referring to my badgering as badgering. I finally let Luther off the hook. Tressel is able to rehabilitate him somewhat on redirect, but the damage has been done.

This is a cross-examination that has gone very well, and I think, for the first time, Tressel knows he's in a fistfight.

I told you Hilda was good," Sam says when he calls after court.

"I like the way this conversation is starting," I say. "What did she find?"

"I put her on Calderone's finances, and she went through all his personal stuff, bank account, credit cards . . . there was nothing unusual."

"This is going to get better, right?" I ask.

"No question about it. She dug deeper, and she found out he's a carpenter, although I think it's more of a handyman. He'll do pretty much any odd job around the house."

"Sam, we don't need our roof repaired, or a toolshed built, and I already knew Calderone was a carpenter. Will you get to the point?"

"I'm about to. He set up a company. It's not a corporation; it's a 'doing business as.' It's called Frankie Do-Right. So Hilda found the bank account for the business, and he received ten thousand dollars around the same time that Hennessey got his twenty-five."

That corresponds to the story Calderone told us in the park. "Who gave him the money?"

"That's the good part. He got a wire from Committee for a Better America, the same people that paid off Hennessey."

"Sam, will you give Hilda a kiss for me?"

"Sure, as long as Eli doesn't mind."

I hang up feeling much better about where we stand. We had a good day in court but a better day after. Our ability to prove that the same people paid large sums of money to both Calderone and Hennessey means that we can establish a firm connection between them.

It is the link we need to bolster Calderone's credibility if we call on him to testify. Now it would not just be his word against Barnett's; there would be solid evidence to back his word up.

My first call is to Hike to ask him to get a subpoena to legally acquire the financial records that Hilda just hacked into. The downside to that is that Tressel will now get Calderone on his radar, but it can't be helped.

My second call is to Laurie, asking her to contact Marcus. I want Calderone in a safe place, where I know I can find him. "Tell Marcus that Big Tiny will know where Calderone is," I say. "We need to find him and put him in a safe place that only we know about. I don't want Tressel getting to him, and I sure don't want Barnett having any idea where he is. But I want to see and talk to him when Marcus has him set up somewhere."

I head home feeling pretty good. No, that's too strong. I head home feeling not as bad as usual. I scored some significant points in court today, though by themselves they couldn't carry the day. But the financial news that Sam and Hilda uncovered gives me an opening to present the case that we're building when it's our turn. That has the potential to be very meaningful.

I offer to take Laurie and Ricky out to dinner, and they jump at it. We go to one of those Japanese hibachi restaurants in Fort Lee, a place we frequent for three basic reasons: (1) We all like the food; (2) Ricky loves to watch the guy cook it at the table; and (3) Laurie likes the fact that the sauce they use gets Ricky and me to eat vegetables, no mean feat. The truth is that the sauce is so good that I'd probably eat horseshit if I could dunk it in that stuff first.

Ricky orders one of those enormous nonalcoholic drinks with all kinds of fruit on a large toothpick. They are still using Santa Claus toothpicks; they must have overordered this year.

It's a really nice meal and family experience, and a good time is had by all. For my part, I spend an entire hour and a half not once thinking about murders, which for me is a rarity.

When we get home, I take Tara and Sebastian for a walk. A lot of our neighbors still have their Christmas lights up; if it was up to me, they could stay up all year. It gives the neighborhood a nice feeling, a literal glow. All of this is a continuation of my relaxed state; I'm not even dreading going through trial documents tonight.

Laurie is in Ricky's room putting him to bed when I get home, and she calls out to me that there's a message on the answering machine. I press the button, and a familiar voice says, "Andy, Walter Tillman. Sorry to bother you at home, but something has come up and we need to talk. I'm still in the office."

Once again, there's that "need to talk" phrase that I hate so much. It never portends anything good. When I rule the kingdom, that phrase will be abolished along with Bing Crosby, and all talk will be voluntary. So it shall be written, and so it shall come to pass.

I call Walter back, and he gets right to the point. "I'm not sure who to blame, you or me, probably me. But we've heard from the prodigal son."

"Hank?" I ask, though I know that's who he means.

"The very one," Tillman says. "Though I didn't speak to him personally, I spoke to one Nolan Weisler, his newly hired attorney."

"Let me guess; they're seeking all or part of dear old dad's estate."

"You're clairvoyant."

"I don't want to jinx this," I say. "But I think we're going to win at trial; there's been a recent development which I am very encouraged about. So all this might be moot." I trust Walter, but I'm keeping Calderone and Barnett's involvement secret all the way.

"I'm very glad to hear that," he says. "But it's become a little more complicated."

"How so?"

"Well, obviously if you lose at trial, young Hank has a very good shot. But Mr. Weisler informs me that in the event of such a development, they will file a civil suit, in an attempt to assign civil responsibility for the murder. They could win a judgment for all or most of the estate if they prevail."

"Smart," I say. It's a situation similar to the O. J. Simpson case. Simpson was acquitted, but the families of the victims brought a civil action against him. That new jury found him responsible for the murders, and they won a huge financial judgment against him.

A civil case is easier to win, since it has a different standard. You just have to demonstrate guilt based on a preponderance of the evidence, rather than beyond a reasonable doubt. Additionally, the verdict does not have to be unanimous. So even if we win the current trial, it would need to be a crushing win to damage Hank's chances in the civil suit.

"Thanks for letting me know," I say. "I'll tell Pups."

"Good. Can you also get her to authorize some pretrial prep, so we'll be ready if there's a civil trial? Also, while I hate to state the obvious, by the time that suit is heard, we may be defending the estate rather than Pups."

He's referring to her short life expectancy, and he's probably right. "I'll discuss it with her," I say. "But much as I don't relish the idea, I would suggest to her that I handle any civil trial or that we do so together. It would essentially be a repeat of the criminal trial, and I obviously am much better versed in the details than you are."

"Whatever she decides is fine with me," Walter says, but he sounds a little miffed. He'll just have to get over it.

I'm over the whole thing as soon as I hang up the phone. I need to focus on tomorrow; I have a trial to win.

**T**ressel calls Katie Nyland as his next witness.

She is the neighbor, or rather the sister of a neighbor, who happened to see Pups come out of Hennessey's house after she discovered the body.

First, he has her reveal that she doesn't exactly live in the neighborhood but was visiting from Oregon. Her younger sister lives next door to Hennessey's house.

"Please describe what happened that night," Tressel says.

"Nothing very unusual. We had run out of milk, and I walked to the convenience store to get it. At home, I always take a long walk after dinner, so that's why I didn't drive."

"So what took place when you returned home?"

"As I was approaching the house next door, Mr. Hennessey's house, I saw that lady come out the front door." She points at Pups.

"Did you recognize her?"

"Yes, I visit two or three times a year, so I've seen her a number of times. My sister even introduced us once."

"Did you and the defendant speak that night, Ms. Nyland?"

"I didn't say anything. But she did. She left the front door of the house open, and when she saw me, she said, 'Don't go in there.' I certainly had no intention of going in there, so it seemed like a strange thing to say."

"What did she do then?"

"She ran to her house and went inside."

"When you say that she 'ran,' do you mean she literally ran?"

"Oh, yes."

"So what did you do then?"

"I went inside my sister's house and told her what had happened. She said not to worry about it, that that woman—she called her 'Pups'—could be strange at times. And then, right after that, there were all these sirens, and the entire street was filled with police."

Tressel turns her over to me, and after thanking her for making the trip back to New Jersey from Oregon in order to testify, I ask her if the street on which her sister lives is a quiet one.

"I think so, yes," she says. "Of course, it depends on what you're comparing it to."

"Was it quiet that night? I mean, while you were walking, before the police started arriving."

"Yes, it was."

"While you were walking, before you saw Ms. Boyer, did you hear anything that might have sounded like a rifle shot?"

"No, I did not."

"How long would you estimate it took from the time you saw Ms. Boyer enter her house and the police arrival?"

"It's hard to say. I wasn't checking my watch, but maybe seven minutes?"

"So if I were to tell you that police records show that the police arrived on the scene four minutes after receiving the 911 call, that would mean it took three minutes for her to make the call?"

"I suppose," she says.

"Could you wash and scrub your hands, change your clothes, and hide the ones you took off in three minutes?"

Tressel explodes out of his chair with an objection, and Chambers correctly sustains it. I've made my point, so I let Ms. Nyland off the stand. She hasn't damaged us in any serious way; we had never contested the fact that Pups discovered the body, and it got some valuable timeline testimony in for us.

Tressel's next witness is an unusual one. He calls Juanita Torres, a court reporter who handled that function at the hearing to deal with Hennessey's original complaint. She had been instructed to bring the transcript of that hearing with her, and Tressel has her read the part where Pups admitted she'd threatened to "cut Hennessey's heart out and shove it down his throat."

After Ms. Torres are a couple of witnesses merely to establish the science. A sergeant in forensics describes in more detail than is necessary exactly how the bullets match up in the various murders, indicating that the same gun, the one in Pups's basement, was used.

Then an assistant coroner testifies that a bullet to the head was in fact the cause of death. That is not exactly a shocker, and I'm quite sure that Tressel only bothered with it so that he could show the jury the gory pictures.

My questions for these witnesses are very brief and merely designed to show the jury that we remain awake. There is nothing to challenge in what they are saying, nor is there much damage being inflicted.

It's near the end of the day that alarm bells start to go off. One of Tressel's assistants comes into court, and Tressel is granted a ten-minute delay to consult with her. When that is concluded, he submits to the court a revised witness list, with one name added. That name is Linda Devereux.

I object that we have not gotten any discovery on Ms. Devereux, but Tressel fends that off by saying that she has just come forward and that, therefore, there are no documents or interviews to turn over.

I turn to Pups and say, "Does that name mean anything to you?"

"Never heard of her. Who could she be?"

"We'll find out tomorrow."

I spent last night trying to figure out who Linda Devereux is, and what she has to do with this case.

More significantly, I had Sam and his computer trying to do the same thing. Neither of us got anywhere. So now all I can do is sit here and wait for her to take the stand; I've got a bad feeling about this one.

Tressel calls her, and she enters the courtroom. She looks to be in her late forties, well dressed and very attractive. She also looks calm and poised, as if she does this every day.

Tressel takes her through a minibiography. Born in western Pennsylvania, graduated Amherst, worked in government in DC for a while, moved to New York, where she worked in the cosmetics industry, married and divorced. She's lived in the Bahamas for the past eighteen months.

"Ms. Devereux, did you know Jake Boyer?"

She nods. "I did. I knew Jake very well."

"Please describe your relationship," he says.

"We were close friends, and then we became lovers. We had an affair that lasted for a little over a year."

I can feel Pups tense up next to me. I can sense her anger, so I take my hand and press it on her leg, in a signal for her to calm down.

"When you say 'affair,' that means you had a physical relationship?"

"Very definitely. But it was much more than that. Jake was a very loving, caring man."

"How often did you see him during the time you were having this affair?"

"Not often enough. I was living in the city, and we used to go upstate, sometimes to Pennsylvania. We'd stay in inns, bed and breakfasts, that kind of thing."

"And eventually you split up?"

She nods. "We did; he broke it off. He said his wife found out and that she was furious. But he couldn't leave her, because she had just been diagnosed with a serious disease— some name I had never heard of."

"But he told you she was angry?"

"Oh, yes. He described it as out of control. But he said he deserved it, that he had hurt her badly, and that he needed to be with her as she fought this disease."

"What did you do when your relationship ended?"

"I was distraught and felt I needed a new start. So I moved to the Bahamas, where I met a wonderful man, and we married a year ago."

"How long after you moved was Jake Boyer murdered?"

"Just about a week. A friend called and told me about it,

said she had read it in the papers. What a terrible thing to happen."

"Did you think that Jake's wife might have been involved?"

She shakes her head. "No, it never entered my mind. They said it was a gang killing and that Jake was just in the wrong place at the wrong time. I assumed that was true. Besides, Jake said that, as angry as his wife was, he believed she still loved him."

"What made you come forward now?" Tressel asks.

"A story about this situation . . . this trial . . . was in our local paper, and I read it. At first, I wasn't going to say anything. I mean, I have a husband and new life, but I felt I had to. If people were saying Jake's wife might have done this, then I thought that what I knew might be important."

This is bad, very bad, and I have a feeling that there is still a bomb to be dropped.

"Ms. Devereux, did Jake Boyer ever give you any gifts?"

"Oh, yes. He was very generous."

"What kind of gifts?"

"Some jewelry, and when we would meet, we'd do things like shop for antiques. Like I said, he was very generous."

"Did he ever give you money?"

"Yes, I'm embarrassed to say that he did. When we broke up and I was moving to the Bahamas, I had very little money and no job waiting for me. He wanted to give me some money to help out. At first, I said no, but then I took it."

"How much?"

"Fifty thousand dollars."

"Did he give you cash?" Tressel asks. "A check?"

"He wired the money into my account."

Tressel walks to the defense table and takes two sheets of paper out of his folder. He gives one to the judge and one to me. "Your Honor, if it please the court, I'd like to introduce this into evidence. It is a copy of Ms. Devereux's bank statement, showing the wire transfer from Jake Boyer to Ms. Devereux."

Double kaboom.

I have no questions for Devereux.

Asking her anything at this point would be violating the tenet that law students learn on day 1: never ask a question that you don't know the answer to.

For all I know, a question of mine could prompt her to pull out a wedding album from the day she and Jake Boyer eloped. It's just too risky; I have to get her off the stand.

I have strong doubt that Tressel was being straight with the court in saying that he just found out about Devereux and that he put her right on the stand when he did. My suspicion is that he knew about her but kept her at arm's length until he felt the time was right.

For the prosecution's case, the timing could not have been more right. Voluntary or not, Tressel finishing his case with her was a brilliant stroke, and I'm sure the jury thinks we are reeling and badly hurt. They're right about that.

So when Tressel turns Devereux over to me, I say that I have no questions for her, but I couch it in a complaint to Chambers that we were blindsided unfairly by not having advance notice of her testimony. I also say that we reserve the right to call her back in our case. Both statements are designed to get the jury not to view our lack of questions now as significant. It's fairly lame, but it's the best I can do.

Tressel rests the prosecution's case, and the smug smile he gives me indicates he thinks it's resting pretty comfortably. Chambers breaks for lunch, instructing me to be ready to call my first witness when we return.

I take Pups into an anteroom and ask her what she knows about Devereux.

"I don't know anything about her," she says. "But I know plenty about Jake. He was the most honest man I've ever met, and he would never lie to me. I know many wives would say that, but it was different between Jake and me. We had a thing between us; we said that if one of us ever wanted out, that would be it, no hard feelings. We said it every year, on January first. She's lying, Andy."

I nod. "OK. We'll deal with her when the time comes." I believe Pups, but I also believed Devereux when she was testifying. The unfortunate thing is that they could both be telling the truth. Devereux could be being honest about the affair, and Pups could honestly believe that she has to be lying.

I let Pups go with the bailiff to get some lunch, but I stay in the room to think and prepare. The damage that Devereux inflicted is considerable, but not fatal. What it did was give Pups a motive to kill Jake, whereas none existed before.

Walter Tillman had testified that their relationship was excellent, without a hint of discord. Devereux says otherwise.

She portrays Pups as a woman horribly scorned at the worst possible time, when she was dealing with a terrible disease and a deadly prognosis.

She has Jake saying that Pups was furious at the betrayal, shortly before he was shot and killed—killed with a gun found in Pups's basement, a year and a half later. And she backs it all up with a bank record showing that Jake gave her fifty thousand dollars.

This is not good.

I can't dwell on this. I'll give Laurie and Sam the task of trying to find something that shakes Devereux's credibility, and if they find anything, I'll put her back on the stand and take her apart. If they don't, I won't.

My focus has to be on presenting our case. If I can get the jury to consider that David Barnett very well might be behind the murders, then it won't matter whether Jake was having an affair.

My first witness is Dr. Cynthia Herrera, Pups's oncologist at Sloan Kettering. I take her through her credentials, both education and employment. This is one impressive woman, which makes sense. You don't get to be a top oncologist at a hospital like that by answering an ad in craigslist.

I then have her describe Pups's condition, malignant meso-thelioma. I had cautioned her in advance to keep it as simple as possible for the jury, and though she tries to do that, she can't quite pull it off. Her testimony starts to get very technical, and I steer her back to the lay world.

"Are you the doctor that gave her the diagnosis?" I ask.

"I was. It's never easy."

"What was her reaction?"

"Remarkable; she took it in stride, at least outwardly. I think having her husband there was comforting to her."

"He was there?" I ask.

"Oh, yes. He was there every time I saw her, until his death."

"How many times was that?"

"Starting with the first visit, it took a number of visits and tests even to make the diagnosis . . . I would say seven or eight times."

"Did he wait out in the waiting area for her most of those times?"

"No, she was very clear that she wanted him with her. And he seemed to want to be there as well."

"Did you notice any discord between them?"

She shakes her head. "On the contrary, they seemed very close. He even called me twice, I believe without her knowledge, to ask what he could do to help make it easier for her."

"Were financial matters a serious factor in the treatment she got?"

"No. She has insurance, but there were and are costs beyond that. Neither of them ever seemed concerned about money."

"Can you think of a reason why a person in her condition, with such a short life expectancy, would want to kill her husband to get his money?"

Tressel objects and Chambers sustains, admonishing me in the process. That's fair, because it was a question that had no chance to get answered. I just wanted to make sure that the jury would hear that a dying woman killing to get money she could never use is a ridiculous concept. I had no way to get the doctor to say it, so I included it in my question.

Tressel's cross-examination begins with, "Doctor, do you consider yourself well trained to deal with a medical condition such as the defendant has?"

"Yes, I do," she says.

"Your entire professional life trained you for situations just like this, correct?"

"Yes."

"And I think I speak for everyone in this courtroom when I say your credentials and training and accomplishments in this area are extraordinarily impressive."

"Thank you," she says.

"Have you had a similar amount of training in the area of detecting cheating husbands?"

"No."

"What about in judging the quality of marriages? How many years of your professional life have you dedicated to that?"

"None."

"Is it within the realm of possibility that after presenting a united front in your office, they went home and argued?"

"Yes."

"Is it even possible that Mr. Boyer was conducting an affair beyond his wife's back?"

"I suppose it is."

"Thank you, Doctor."

It's getting late, and Chambers asks me if I want to call

another witness now or adjourn for the weekend. I choose the latter. It's been an up-or-down week, but it's all been just the preliminary round.

Next week is the key.

If there's one thing I have learned, it's that Big Tiny Parker can be counted on.

That's comforting, because if you can't count on vicious gang leaders, then who can you count on?

Marcus told Big Tiny that I needed Calderone, and he found him very quickly. For all I know, he might have had one of his people watching him all this time. I don't think he did it because he's fond of me or even because he's afraid of Marcus. He did it because he wants to find his brother's killer. Big Tiny's interests are aligned with mine. That's a good thing.

Marcus picks me up and takes me to where Calderone is staying, although there is a thin line between "staying" and "held captive." It's a cabin just south of White Meadow Lake, which is simultaneously twenty-five minutes and light-years away from Paterson.

The cabin is somehow owned or used by either Big Tiny or the Bloodz, and it is set in the woods well off the road. I don't know why the gang has it or what they use it for, and I certainly don't want to know.

When we arrive, Calderone is inside with Big Tiny and two of his guys, including, I think, one of the guys Marcus dispatched at the bar. But I'd just as soon not chat about old times.

The cabin is actually quite comfortable and even gets satellite TV. Calderone looks fairly relaxed and unthreatened, which I'm pleased about. The less he looks like a frightened basket case, the better witness he will be.

"You doing OK?" I ask Calderone.

"Super. What a way to spend a Saturday night."

"You ready to testify tomorrow?"

"Do I have a choice?" he asks.

"I can't force you," I say.

Calderone points to Big Tiny. "You can't, but he can. He told me if I don't do what you say, he'll slice me open from front to back like a fish."

I smile. "He's a real kidder, that Big Tiny."

"You know Barnett is going to kill me," Calderone says.

I shake my head. "No, he isn't. You and I are going to put him away."

"He's got friends," he says.

I point around the room at the three gang guys and Marcus. "So do you."

I quickly go over his testimony with him; there isn't that much to cover, and all I want him to do is tell the truth as he told it to me. I'm pleasantly surprised by his demeanor; I think he'll do fine.

As I'm about to leave, I ask no one in particular, "Do we have a plan to get him to court at nine AM Monday?"

"He'll be there," Big Tiny says. "Don't worry about it."

Marcus and I drive back. The lack of conversation in the car is good, since it allows me to go over what I plan to cover with Calderone on the stand and with Barnett after that. There is no doubt in my mind that Calderone will make an effective witness, at least to the extent that he will put major suspicions about Barnett in the jury's mind. After that, it will be up to me to dismantle Barnett on the stand.

When I get home, I call Hike to confirm that a process server has served Barnett with a subpoena to appear in court Monday. Hike says that he's received the written notification that it was, in fact, successfully served.

Since we've also legally received the financial information that Sam hacked illegally, everything is in place.

Caffey knew all the players from that night in the park.

He didn't know why they were in the out-of-the-way cabin or whether Calderone was being held there against his will. The good news for Caffey was that it didn't matter what he knew; he wasn't paid to know things.

Caffey had been given prior instructions about what to do in this situation, which was obviously anticipated. He drove to David Barnett's house, parked down the block, and walked in the shadows, unseen until he got there.

He went around the back and knocked on the door. Within moments, Barnett saw it was him and opened the door.

"Why are you here?" he asked

"I'm reporting in; there have been developments."

"Why didn't you call?"

"Because the situation is rapidly changing," Caffey said.

"What do you mean?"

"They have Calderone in a cabin, about a half hour from here."

"Who are they?" Barnett asked.

"Three of the gang members. Then they had a visit tonight from Carpenter and his bodyguard. Based on their behavior, I would say that whatever is going on, they are all in accord about it."

Barnett nodded. "Calderone is going to testify on Monday morning. They're using him to set me up. I need to think about this." Then, "Can you get to him?"

"I can get to anyone," Caffey said.

"Then it's time for our friend to disappear."

"I understand, friend."

It struck Barnett as a strange thing for Caffey to say, but it became somewhat clearer when he saw the gun in his hand.

"What the hell are you doing?"

"I'm following instructions. Let's go."

"You get your instructions from me."

"Not this time," Caffey said, raising the gun slightly. "This comes from higher up."

**S**unday comes at a good time this week.

I walk Tara and Sebastian and then have breakfast with Ricky and Laurie. A typical American start to a Sunday morning, except for the part where I go to the prison after breakfast.

I haven't had much chance to talk to Pups since the devastating Devereux testimony, and I feel like I should. Unfortunately, I have nothing good to tell her so far, since Laurie and Sam have come up empty in the early stages of their investigation.

Devereux's description of her biography and current living conditions was accurate, and so far we can't confirm or deny the affair with Jake. It's very hard to prove a negative, especially since if the affair was real, the parties would have made efforts to shield it.

I tell her all this, but she dismisses it with, "It doesn't matter what you find or don't find. She was lying."

She obviously has complete faith in her late husband, and

I see no reason to try to shake it. "I've got more news for you," I say.

"You'd better; you're screwing up my whole Sunday."

I smile; she's as big a wiseass in prison as she was when she had her freedom. "Unfortunately, it's not news you're going to like very much."

"Just tell me already," she says.

"OK. Jake's son, Hank, is going to go after your estate."

"You've got to be kidding. Can he do that?"

"He can certainly go after it. Whether he can get it depends on circumstances. If you're convicted of murdering Jake, then legally you cannot receive the proceeds of his will. Hank would have an excellent argument for being next in line."

"Even though Jake left him out entirely?"

"I'm afraid so. But that's OK, because we're in the process of seeing to it that you're not convicted."

She shakes her head. "The twerp wants nothing to do with his father's life, but he wants to jump all over his death."

I don't mention to Pups that I brought Hank into the picture; she'd probably kill me, which would necessitate another trial. "Unfortunately," I say, "an acquittal doesn't end it."

"Why not?"

"He's also filing a civil suit for wrongful death, claiming you are responsible for Jake's death. In that case, he's not going after the will but, rather, your estate. Which essentially is the same thing."

"How can I be responsible if I've already been found innocent?"

"It's a different standard. In a civil case, the standard is not reasonable doubt but, rather, preponderance of the evidence. And the jury's verdict would not have to be unanimous. For example, O. J. Simpson was acquitted criminally but found responsible civilly."

"You lawyers are a pain in the ass," she says.

"I'm aware of that. Next item . . . Walter Tillman is asking if you want him to represent you, should there be a civil trial. If so, he needs to start preparing, and there will be some costs involved."

"But it would be a murder trial, like this one?"

"Essentially, with some differences in legal procedure. But yes."

"Then I want you."

She's right that I should handle it; I'm totally immersed in the facts of the case already. Walter will ultimately understand as well, and may even be relieved. "OK," I say. "I'll see you tomorrow; it's going to be a big day."

Sam and Hike are waiting for me at home so they can report on what they have learned about Jake's various land holdings, which are now owned by Pups.

"There's not a lot here," Sam says. "That's because if there is something, it obviously hasn't been made public. If somebody is sitting in Nebraska knowing that on Pups's land there is a huge titanium deposit, we'd have no way of knowing that."

"I understand," I say.

"There are three possible situations, but I can't say I have much confidence in any of them," Sam says. "The first is land in Montana; there have been rumors for years of gold deposits in the area, but very little has ever been found. Prospectors apparently show up there every once in a while, sure that they are going to make a killing, but never seem to."

"This is on Pups's land?"

"Hers is a large parcel in the area. Hard to know if prospectors have trespassed on it or not."

"What's number two?" I ask.

"Her largest parcel is in South Dakota. North Dakota produces a huge amount of oil through fracking, and they need to get it to refineries in Louisiana. They've been sending it by rail, but pipelines would be much more efficient."

"Like the Keystone pipeline?"

Hike speaks up. "Yeah, but without as much controversy. This isn't coming from Canada, so it's going to get done. But even with that, it's been tied up for a couple of years, waiting for environmental impact statements and stuff."

"And they'll have to go on Pups's land?" I ask.

Hike shakes his head. "No, there are a few ways to do it, if they do it at all. It's in committee in the South Dakota legislature, and the committee will decide. But there's another route that's considered the big favorite."

"How about number three?" I ask, feeling less hopeful each time.

"There's talk of building a planned community in Nevada. It would be the fourth big gambling area in the state and would be built somewhere between Vegas and Reno/Tahoe. But they have a lot of options besides Pups's land, and it's probably years away anyway."

"OK. Good work, guys. Keep an eye on this as best you can, Sam, especially the oil-pipeline one. That's the most interesting to me."

"Will do."

I send them off and head for the den to prepare. As I told Pups, big day tomorrow.

**C**alderone is dressed in a pretty decent suit for his court appearance.

I have no idea where he got it. It's certainly not Big Tiny's; if Big Tiny owned a suit, you could fit two Calderones in it, with room for me and Ricky.

Court is late starting today, because one of the jurors had a medical issue. All it means is that the lunch break will separate Calderone's testimony from Barnett's, which is not a big deal either way.

I start off with Calderone by taking him through his history, such as it is. He made it through two years of high school, married young, divorced soon after, no kids.

"Have you ever been in prison?" I ask.

He nods. "Twice. For a total of three and a half years."

"What was the crime you were convicted of?"

"Breaking and entering," he says.

"Were you guilty?"

"The juries said I was."

"Were they right?"

He thinks for a moment and then shrugs, apparently deciding no damage would be done. "Yeah. I was guilty."

"Did you ever have occasion to meet Randall Hennessey?" I ask.

"Yes."

"How did that come about?"

"Someone asked me to talk to him," he says. "He wanted me to get Hennessey to complain about her dogs." He points to Pups. "I was supposed to offer him twenty-five thousand dollars to do it."

"Who made the request?"

"David Barnett."

"Did you know him before he approached you to do this?"

"I did some carpentry work for him at his house. We talked some; he knew my background."

I nod. "Did you think you were doing anything illegal?"

He shrugs. "I figured he had something going on, but all I was doing was asking somebody to complain about some dogs. I didn't see where that was breaking any law."

He goes on to say that he spoke to Hennessey to confirm that the complaint was made and to further confirm the payments.

"Your Honor," I say, taking documents from Hike, "I would like to submit this into evidence. It shows wire transfers from an online bank, from an account with the name Committee for a Better America. There are two wires, payable to Mr. Hennessey. One is for fifteen thousand, made just before the complaint was filed to the zoning board. The other is for ten thousand dollars, sent just after the complaint was filed."

"Were you yourself paid for talking to Mr. Hennessey?"

He nods. "Ten thousand dollars."

I introduce into evidence bank records showing that the same group wired Calderone his money, from the same bank. I also introduce the phone records showing that Hennessey and Calderone had three phone calls between them.

"Did you ever ask Mr. Barnett why he was paying all this money for something like this?"

"No, I just wanted my money. I didn't want to know."

"What did you think when you heard that Mr. Hennessey was subsequently killed?" I ask.

"Then I really didn't want to know."

I finish with Calderone, hoping the jury will understand that the matching bank statements give his testimony way more credibility than he would otherwise have. I'll need to put the finishing touches on it by nailing Barnett when I have him on the stand. When I go back to the defense table, I'm surprised to see that Hike is not there.

Tressel gets up to cross-examine Calderone, and his attitude is one of almost bemusement, as if this is so ridiculous and irrelevant as to be beneath him.

"Mr. Calderone, your testimony is that Mr. Barnett paid you ten thousand dollars to have a conversation with Mr. Hennessey?"

"Yes."

"Are you a really good conversationalist?"

"I am, when I'm told what to say." It's such a good answer that I want to stand up and cheer.

"How long did your initial conversation with Mr. Hennessey take?"

"About forty-five minutes. He couldn't believe it."

Tressel nods. "That's understandable. So with your later conversations, you put in about two hours' work for your ten thousand dollars?"

"Right."

"Did Mr. Hennessey report you to any authorities for this? Did he try and get you in trouble?"

"No."

"Because you did nothing wrong, correct?"

"Correct."

"Then why didn't Mr. Barnett just talk to him himself and save the ten grand?"

"I don't know," he says, as I object on the grounds that he couldn't know.

"But you are willing to say things for money?" Tressel asks.

"Depends on the things and depends on the money."

"Mr. Calderone, do you have any proof, any evidence, to demonstrate that all of this happened as you say? That you were put up to it by Mr. Barnett?"

"No."

"Any proof you talked Mr. Hennessey into filing the complaint?"

"No."

"Thank you. No further questions."

Chambers adjourns for the lunch break as Hike comes back into the courtroom. I don't like the look on his face. "What's the matter?" I ask.

"Barnett never showed up."

**A**t the moment there is nothing of consequence that I can do.

I ask the court staff if they've heard from Barnett today, perhaps to give an excuse for his nonattendance. None of them have.

Hike contacts the process server who served the subpoena on Barnett, compelling his testimony today. The man is going to go back out to Barnett's house, but it will be a while before he reports back.

We wait out the lunch break, but still no Barnett. When Judge Chambers starts the afternoon session, I ask that we discuss an issue before the jury is brought back in.

"Judge, our next witness is David Barnett. As you know, he was subject to recall, and we served him with a lawful subpoena compelling his appearance in court at this time."

I give Chambers a copy of the subpoena and then continue. "He has failed to appear, and efforts to reach him have so far been unsuccessful. As you can imagine, this testimony is the linchpin to our case; we believe that Mr. Barnett is culpable for these murders. I am speculating now, but that could be the reason for his fleeing, if that is in fact what he has done."

"What are you requesting of the court?" Chambers asks.

"A continuance, at least until we can determine what has happened here."

"Mr. Tressel?"

Tressel stands to respond. There is slightly more than a 100 percent chance that he will be opposed to the request. "Your Honor, I don't see why Mr. Carpenter can't call a different witness now and put Mr. Barnett on the stand when he is found."

I shake my head. "That doesn't work for two reasons. First, there is a momentum to the case. I would have thought Mr. Tressel would be aware of this, but the order in which witnesses testify is not scattershot; it is strategic. But more important, I was planning to question Mr. Barnett for the rest of the day. I have no other witnesses here today."

Chambers's hands are effectively tied. He can't force me to call a witness if there are none here, and he can't penalize me for Barnett not showing up. I went through the proper procedure to get him here.

"I'll grant the continuance until nine o'clock tomorrow."

"Your Honor, can you also instruct law enforcement to join the effort to find Mr. Barnett?"

He nods. "I will certainly do that."

Judge Chambers adjourns the session but directs that the lawyers remain within the vicinity of the courthouse, so we can reconvene quickly if Barnett shows up. I don't think that is going to happen. Barnett struck me as a pretty buttoned-down guy; I can see him not showing up at all more easily than I can see him just wandering in late. He's also smart enough to know that a subpoena is not something to be trifled with.

Three hours go by, and Hike and I just sit there and wait. I've got a lot of reasons to despise Barnett; I think he caused the murder of three people and put Pups in the awful situation she's in. But taking its place at the top of the list is his causing me to spend three hours alone with Hike.

The word finally comes down that we are to meet in private session with Judge Chambers. It's just lead counsel, which means me, Tressel, Chambers, and a court reporter. But there is another person there when I arrive, Detective Nicholas Summers, who, I assume, is there to report on the brief search that has been conducted for Barnett.

I've had some dealings with Summers in the past. He's smart and fair, like most detectives I've met, and he dislikes me, like all detectives I've met.

Summers reports that Barnett is indeed nowhere to be found but that there are signs that he left his house hurriedly and carelessly. The front door of the house was ajar, and a flame was still lit on the stove under what might have been a pot of boiling water.

Significantly, his two cars remain in his garage, giving the impression that, when he left, he did not leave alone. "Of course," Summers says, "there is no way at this point to know if the other person was aiding him or was an adversary."

"What's your best guess?" I ask.

"An adversary. I'm going on very little information here,

but my hunch is that he was abducted. It's a strong enough hunch for me to have labeled this a missing persons case, even though he has not been gone long enough for such a designation to usually kick in."

Chambers asks, "Do we know when he went missing?"

Summers shakes his head. "No, although no neighbors saw him yesterday. They said that when he is home on a Sunday, he's always out to some degree, usually walking. Also, the Sunday newspapers had not been brought in, and no phone calls were made from his landline either. So the working theory is Saturday night, though that's just informed speculation at this point."

I turn to Chambers. "Your Honor, the jury needs to be instructed that they can draw a negative inference from this if they wish."

Tressel jumps in, sensing disaster. "That's absurd," he says. "The police admit that everything is speculation at this point, but the jury is in a position to draw conclusions?"

"Mr. Tressel is missing the point, Your Honor," I say. "The speculation the detective was talking about concerned whether Mr. Barnett has fled or been abducted. Either of those two choices is worthy of a negative inference being drawn."

I continue. "We have just presented a witness that implicated Mr. Barnett in these crimes. If he suddenly decided to flee a lawful subpoena, that's hardly a coincidence. If he were abducted, the same thing holds. He could well have been removed by accomplices concerned with being brought down by Mr. Barnett's testimony."

I continue. "The third possibility, that he suddenly took this moment to take a vacation, leaving boiling water behind, is too ridiculous to seriously consider."

Tressel shakes his head. "We need to deal with facts, Your Honor. There could be a fourth or fifth possibility that we haven't even thought about. It is dangerous and perhaps unprecedented to have the jury concocting scenarios in their own mind."

Chambers says, "We'll adjourn and reconvene at ten AM tomorrow morning, at which point, assuming Mr. Barnett hasn't materialized, I will issue a directive to the jury. Detective, please provide me with an update no later than nine AM."

Summers agrees, and we end our little get-together.

The day hadn't gone quite as I expected.

**B**arnett's absence might not be a disaster.

The key will be how clear I can make it to the jury that his unavailability is consistent with guilt. Much of that will be up to the judge, but if he gives me some leeway, I think I can be effective. When the jury hears that someone has run away, they will want to know the reason.

If I had to guess, I would think that Barnett is no longer among the living. His situation was not so dire that a smart guy like him would have run; even getting Pups acquitted would be light-years away from getting him convicted.

I never saw him as the trigger man, anyway; I saw him as part of a financial conspiracy that hired the shooter to do their bidding. It seems likely that his partners decided that he represented a risk to them, that if he went down, he might bring them with him.

I head back to the office to pick up some files, and there is a message on my phone from Nolan Weisler. He identifies himself as the local attorney for Hank Boyer and wants to have a preliminary conversation before they file the civil suit accusing Pups of the wrongful death of her husband, Hank's father.

I would rather have a heaping plate of steamed broccoli than talk to this guy, but I know I'm going to have to eventually, so I call him to get it behind me.

He gives me a pleasant enough hello and thanks me for calling, and then he says that he understands from Walter Tillman that I will be representing Martha Boyer in the civil case.

"That's correct," I say. "Have you filed your suit yet?"

"No. My client instructed me to pursue the possibility of a settlement. He doesn't think a trial benefits anyone, especially with your client's medical condition."

"His concern brings tears to my eyes," I say.

"No need to bring sarcasm into this discussion," he says.

"Sarcasm for me is an annoyance reducer," I say. "I'm using it in this case because your client is an annoyance."

"From what I have been able to ascertain, he is an annoyance with a strong case. In any event, I don't want to further irritate you. Are you interested in settlement talks or not? I have seen the estate as listed in Jake Boyer's will, so I am prepared to make a fair offer."

I want to tell him to shove his offer, because I know Pups will tell me to do the same, but I catch myself just in time. I want to see his offer, in the unlikely but possible event that he has found the hidden value I suspect is there.

"Yes, definitely make your offer. My client will give it every consideration."

He thanks me and tells me that I will receive it by FedEx

tomorrow. Since I have no witnesses to question, it will give me something to do.

In the meantime, I head down to Charlie's, where I know Vince Sanders and Pete will be watching the Knicks game. Once they get over their surprise that I'm there and their relief that they won't have to pay the check, I tell Vince that I have a scoop for him.

"I live for your scoops," he says. "My whole life is planned around receiving your scoops. Talk to me at halftime."

"Here's your headline," Pete says. "Carpenter's client to be convicted, but Carpenter still collects fee."

I ignore Pete and tell Vince, "I won't be here at halftime. You want it or not? It will be front-page news; the four readers you have left will eat it up."

"There may only be four," Vince says, "but they're loyal as hell. What have you got?"

I tell him about Barnett's being missing, emphasizing that it's the defense theory that he is either the murderer or part of the conspiracy.

"Missing?" Vince asks. "Meaning he skipped town?"

"Or something worse. The police are investigating, and there's a chance they'll find out the truth since Pete is not on the case."

"Who's on it?" Pete asks, interested enough to ignore my attack.

"Summers."

Pete nods. "Good detective. Not in my class, but pretty damn good."

Vince picks up his cell phone and calls in the story to his

city desk, or wherever it is that editors call when they have breaking news. The way media works in this day and age, everybody else will have the story before the paper even hits the streets, or the Web site.

Jurors are told never to read about the cases they're involved with, so I always assume that they voraciously devour every bit of news they can find. That is especially true in a situation like this, where the trial has been mysteriously put on hold, without anyone telling them why.

Having accomplished my goal, I tell the waitress to put the food and beverage charge on my tab, and I head home. I've been spending way less time than I'd like with Laurie and Ricky, and although Ricky will be in bed, it will be nice to see and talk to Laurie.

Ricky is sound asleep, so I sneak in and kiss him good night. Laurie is also in bed, our bed, so I speed up the Tara-Sebastian walk a little in order to more quickly join her. She's reading a thriller by David Rosenfelt, one of the great writers of our time, but she puts it down when I get into bed.

"I finally got the definitive answer from Ricky about the last-name situation," she says.

"Uh-oh. What did he say?"

"Well, Rubenstein is still his first choice, but I convinced him that it was a bad idea, that the teachers would get confused with two Rubensteins in the class."

I nod. "That's a very legitimate concern."

"I thought you'd agree," she says. "His second choice is Carpenter."

I've got to be careful here and pretend to be a gracious winner. It's not a role that comes naturally to me. "Ah," I say, a meaningless sound if ever there was one.

She disregards it and continues. "So I've decided to disavow my entire life's identity, my standing as a unique and separate individual, and become Carpenter as well. My son and I should have the same last name."

I need some help here. Every possible response I'm coming up with is going to get me in trouble. "Are you sure about this?" I finally say. "You sound as if you have some slight reservations."

"Wow," she says. "You really are insightful. You see right through me. I feel naked."

"That was my hope when I came in here."

She ignores that and says, "So I'm going to be Laurie Collins-Carpenter, and our son will be Ricky Diaz-Carpenter. You should get started on legally changing the names."

I nod. "And the whole naked thing?"

"No chance."

**J**udge Chambers calls us in for a precourt session.

The players are the same: Tressel, Summers, me, the judge, and the court reporter. I'm quite sure that Summers has already given Chambers the update on the Barnett situation, and we have been brought in to hear it.

"OK, gentlemen, I'm going to make this short and sweet. Detective Summers informs me that Mr. Barnett remains missing and is unlikely to return. He has missed some scheduled meetings, in addition to his court appearance, and has failed to meet some other personal obligations. Detective Summers believes this to be an involuntary disappearance, but, whether voluntary or not, it seems certain that we will have to proceed without him."

"Your Honor," I start, but the judge cuts me off.

"I must say that I was distressed to see this issue in this morning's newspaper. Which of you was responsible for that?"

"That was me, Your Honor," I say. "I felt it was newsworthy, and my hope was that it would turn up information as to Barnett's whereabouts. He is very important to my case."

"He wanted the jury to see it," Tressel says, accurately.

I shake my head. "The jury has been specifically instructed not to read, watch, or listen to anything related to this case."

Chambers is not interested in this byplay, though I'm sure he knows that Tressel is right. He hadn't prohibited contact with the media, so he can't sanction me for it now. "See you in court, gentlemen. Mr. Carpenter, be prepared to call a witness."

As for what the judge will tell the jury, we're not going to know until we know. As we're leaving, I pull Detective Summers aside and ask him if he can hang around for ten minutes. "What for?" he asks.

"It has to do with this case, and it's important. That's all I can say right now." He looks dubious, so I add, "Just ten minutes. Please. Take a seat anywhere in the courtroom."

We head into court and take our seats, with the judge just moments behind us. He calls in the jury and speaks to them. "Ladies and gentlemen, the defense had at this time intended to call as their next witness Mr. Barnett, who you'll remember testified in the prosecution case and was subject to recall. Mr. Barnett has failed to appear, and we have been unable to locate him at this time. Mr. Carpenter, call your next witness."

That was completely unsatisfactory, and in my view so egregious that it might give me an opportunity for appeal. But I don't want to appeal; I want to win. "Defense calls Detective Nicholas Summers."

Tressel jumps out of his chair as if it caught fire. "Objection, Your Honor."

Before he even gets a chance to state the reason for the objection, Chambers calls both of us up to a sidebar at the bench. "Let's hear it, Mr. Carpenter."

"Your Honor, Mr. Barnett is crucial to our case. The jury has seen him testify, and they have just heard from a witness whose testimony incriminated him. Detective Summers has information relevant to his situation and, therefore, relevant to this trial. I can refer you to appeals court decisions that are on point and favor our position."

The last part was a through-my-teeth lie; I don't have the slightest clue if an appeals court has ever addressed this issue. I just want Judge Chambers to think about and be worried about being overturned on appeal. Judges hate that.

Tressel won't have it. "Judge, you obviously made a decision not to tell the jury that they can draw a negative inference from Barnett's disappearance. This does exactly that."

I shake my head. "Wrong again. They are not being told to draw an inference; they are being given facts, which they can weigh along with all the other facts that have made up this trial."

I think I have the judge in a corner, but cornered judges can be dangerous. Fortunately, not this time. "He can testify," Chambers says, and we go back to our seats.

Summers takes the stand, and I ask him why he has been searching for Barnett. "Because the judge asked for police involvement," he says.

"Did Mr. Barnett fail to appear after being served a lawful subpoena?"

"Yes."

I take him through the various things that he found in his investigation: the flame on the stove, the missed meetings, the failure to bring in the Sunday paper or to be seen in the neighborhood—all of it. "In your experience, Detective, do signs like these generally mean that the disappearance is involuntary?"

"It can go either way." He's pissed at me for calling him, so he doesn't want to give me what I want.

"Did you say fifteen minutes ago, in a meeting we just held, that your belief was that it was, in fact, involuntary?"

He can't lie, especially since the court reporter had gotten it down, so he says, "Yes."

"Have you learned anything in the last fifteen minutes that changed your view?"

"No."

Tressel conducts a brief cross, during which he gets Summers to admit that there could be other explanations. "He could have had an accident, or a heart attack, or any one of many other things?" Tressel asks.

"Anything is possible," Summers says, and is finally allowed to get off the stand and go back to work. He'll continue looking for Barnett, but I'll be very surprised if he finds him.

really have very little case left to present.

My strategy was to impeach Tressel's witnesses as much as possible and then point to Barnett as a credible alternative killer. I think I've accomplished both, but I can't really be sure. Certainly, I'm going to have to hammer home my points in my summation.

Pups wants to take the stand, but I am absolutely opposed to it. All she can do is profess her innocence and declare that there is no way Jake could have been having that affair. All of that would be seen as self-serving and not particularly compelling; she has no evidence to back up either assertion.

Even more important is the fact that she would be a time bomb under cross-examination. Tressel would badger her and get her angry, and there is no telling what she might say. Pups is not a delicate flower.

To her credit, even though I admit that she has the absolute right to testify, she honors our agreement at the beginning of the trial that I would call all the shots. So I finish up the defense case with our final two witnesses.

The first is a vice president of the bank where Randall Hennessey had his account. His testimony confirms that the twenty-five thousand dollars wired to Hennessey was the only time he had anywhere close to that much money. In fact, he reveals, those were the only two wire transfers Hennessey ever received.

As our final witness, I call Dierdre Milone, Pups's self-described closest friend in the world.

Laurie has interviewed Dierdre, and I have not, but Laurie tells me what she'll say, and the demeanor with which she'll say it. She turns out to be right, and Dierdre describes Pups as a wonderful person who has devoted her life to unwanted animals.

She was also a close friend of Jake's, and she testifies that the Boyers had a great marriage, that Jake never would have cheated, and that, if he had, Pups would have confided in her about it.

Tressel's cross is relatively brief, as if dismissing her as unimportant. He gets her to say that while she believes all these things, it's impossible to be positive about any of them. If one is not in the marriage, she is forced to admit, it's always possible that it could not be what it seems.

Overall, she is a good witness, and a nice way to end the case.

I utter the toughest words I ever have to say during a trial. Because once I say them, there is no going back. If I later realize that I should have done something differently or called another witness, it's too late.

"Your Honor, the defense rests."

I make a motion that I be allowed to reopen the defense case if David Barnett appears before the jury begins their deliberations. Judge Chambers says that he will hold off making a ruling on that until the situation presents itself, and then he sets closing arguments for tomorrow morning.

I'm sure that I prepare for closing arguments differently from most lawyers, in that I hardly prepare at all. I lay out in my mind what points I am going to cover, but I don't write anything out or practice a set speech.

By this time in the trial, I know the facts and can recall them at will, and I don't want to do anything that detracts from the spontaneity of what I will say. I understand why others do it more by the book, but my way has always worked for me.

I head for the office, and waiting for me is the FedEx package that Nolan Weisler, Hank Boyer's attorney, promised he would send. It contains an offer, specific to the point that it's eleven pages long, detailing a proposed settlement.

I look at it briefly, but spend long enough to determine that Weisler obviously had access to Jake's will, which is, of course, part of the public record. He seems to have asked for half of Pups's liquid assets and has divided up the land as well.

Hike comes into the office to do some paperwork, and I call Sam and ask him to come in too. Edna, with a remarkable burst of energy, makes copies of the offer for Sam and Hike. She doesn't collate them, because there is a limit to what one person can do.

Once they have it in front of them, I say, "I just looked at this quickly, but the land is divided up by parcels. No pieces of land appear to be split; each entire parcel winds up with either Pups or Jake. So the first thing I want you to do is determine which of the three parcels you had isolated previously as potential sources of hidden value are listed in this proposal as going to Jake."

Hike has already been looking through it as I talk. "The Nevada and Nebraska pieces stay with Pups. The South Dakota piece goes to Jake."

"That's the one with the potential pipeline on it?"

Hike nods. "Yes."

"That's the one I thought was the most likely. Let's dig even more deeply into that one. Hike, there's a chance I might want you to go out there and snoop around, see what you can learn."

"To South Dakota?" he asks, his displeasure evident.

I nod. "Unless the land gets moved. Best to go wherever the land is. Sam, I also want you to take all the pieces of land that are on Jake's side in this offer, and go over them again, just in case there's something you missed the first time."

I leave them to their work and head home. I have absolutely no evidence to make me believe that Hank Boyer is part of any conspiracy. I was the one who notified him of his possible inheritance, long after the murders were committed. His going after it, especially with the obvious prodding from his wife, makes perfect sense and is not obviously sinister.

But I have no other answer. My theory is that everything that has transpired has been part of an effort to get Jake's, and then Pups's, money. There are a very limited number of places for that money to ultimately go. It either stays with Pups, goes to the rescue groups as specified in her will, goes to the state of New Jersey, or goes to Hank. Maybe the bad guys have figured out a way to take it away from Hank after he gets it, but that seems unlikely and could not have been their initial plan.

This entire case has revealed an enormous, expensive, deadly conspiracy. No one undertakes that unless there is a huge amount of money at stake and they have a sure way to get it.

**D**an Tressel put on a dark suit and a solemn face to give his closing statement.

His manner said that he was saddened by this whole thing and sorry to be a part of it. But there was a job to do; the public had to be protected.

"Ladies and gentlemen, when this trial started, I stood before you, as I am doing today, and made an opening statement. I told you that your job was to listen intently to all the witnesses that would come before you, to make sure you understood all the different aspects of the case. You have obviously done your job.

"My mandate was to present the facts, without prejudice, so that you could make the proper judgment when the time came for you to deliberate. I hope I have done my job . . . I think I have . . . because your deliberations will come soon.

"Back then I told you that I would prove to you, beyond a reasonable doubt, that Martha Boyer committed three murders. I didn't say that she pulled the trigger in each case but, rather, that she was responsible for all of them happening.

I told you that the murder of her husband, Jake Boyer, was so callous that she ordered the murder of another person, Raymond Parker, simply to throw the police off the track.

"I hope and believe that I have proven all of that to you.

"Jake Boyer was having an affair; he was cheating on his wife. I don't defend that; I simply state it as a fact. But one never knows what's going on inside someone else's marriage, and no one other than Martha and Jake Boyer knew what was going on inside theirs. And whatever he was doing, he did not deserve to die for it.

"You've heard testimony about that affair and seen a financial document that proves it. The defense has not even bothered to claim otherwise. You've heard that Jake told Martha about it and that she was furious. And, soon after that, he was dead.

"You've also heard that Randall Hennessey complained about Martha Boyer, his neighbor, having more than twenty dogs in her house, when the law allowed only three. We don't know why he complained—maybe he didn't like the barking or maybe there was a smell. We'll never know exactly why, because he made Martha Boyer angry, and now he is gone.

"He angered her, she publicly threatened him, he was shot with a gun found moments after the crime in her house, and she was spotted fleeing the murder scene. This is not a whodunit.

"We might never have known who killed Jake Boyer and Raymond Parker had not the same gun been used to kill Randall Hennessey. The defense would have you believe that using the same gun was so ill advised as to be evidence that Martha Boyer must have been framed, that she could not be that stupid or careless.

"But understand this: she did not expect the gun to be found. And if it was found in her possession, then she would be arrested and convicted for the murder of Mr. Hennessey, so what was the difference if those other murders were added on? She was ill; she would die soon anyway.

"I also told you back at the beginning of this trial to not let your sympathy for Martha Boyer's illness sway you. People get sick and die every day, but they don't go on a murder spree before they pass. Jake Boyer and Raymond Parker and Randall Hennessey never had the chance to see where their lives would take them. Martha Boyer saw to that.

"This is your chance to tell Martha Boyer, to tell the citizens of New Jersey, that there is no excuse for cold-blooded murder."

Tressel nods sadly, throwing in a little shake of the head to drive it home, and then says, "Thank you for listening."

As I'm about to get up, Pups leans over to me, to offer a word of encouragement.

Or not.

"The little prick," she says, right on target, as always.

I begin with, "If you'll indulge me, let me tell you what I think you need to do, what I think your job requires. You need to look at the evidence, all of it, and decide if you think Martha Boyer committed these murders beyond a reasonable doubt.

"You must, by definition, find that it is unreasonable to

believe that someone else did it and unreasonable to believe that there is another explanation beyond Mr. Tressel's. Because you cannot have more than one theory of the case and believe either one of them beyond a reasonable doubt.

"You heard the police detective that ran the investigation almost two years ago sit here and tell you that Martha Boyer could not have been on the scene, that she could not have pulled the trigger. His reason? He knew with certainty where she was; she was playing bridge with her friends. And, smart detective that he is, he knew she could not be in two places at once.

"So if she is guilty of those crimes, then she had to have arranged for the killings. She had to have hired someone to do the murdering for her. And it had to be an excellent, experienced shooter; it was dark, he was shooting from a slowly moving car, and he had to hit two different people accurately enough to kill them.

"I've never conducted a survey of hit men, but I'll bet you that if I did, I'd find that the percentage of them that own guns is somewhere between ninety-nine and one hundred and one. Plumbers own plungers; painters own brushes; accountants own pencils; and hit men own guns.

"So what did this hit man do? According to Mr. Tressel's theory of the case, he either borrowed Martha Boyer's gun and then gave it back or used his own gun but gave it to her afterwards as a memento to commemorate the occasion. Not only are both of those explanations unreasonable; they are ridiculous.

"Then he would have you believe that Martha used the

same gun to kill Mr. Hennessey. Then she called the police to the scene, somehow cleaned all traces of gun residue from her hands and clothes in just a few minutes, and put the gun in her basement. But first she wiped her prints from the gun, as if having it in her basement would not be incriminating enough.

"That scenario is, at the very least, unreasonable.

"But someone killed those people; that's something we can all agree on. And we believe that the killer—not necessarily the shooter, but the person who ordered it—was David Barnett.

"David Barnett went with Jake Boyer to the scene of his execution that night, the Bonfire Restaurant. He knew where they would be, and he was obviously, therefore, in a position to tell the shooter. In the hail of bullets that followed, Barnett emerged unscathed, a happy coincidence for him.

"You heard testimony from Frank Calderone, a man who had done work for Barnett. He said that Barnett paid him ten thousand dollars to get Randall Hennessey to complain about Martha Boyer's dogs by promising him twenty-five thousand dollars.

"Now I can see why you might be initially skeptical of this; Frank Calderone is not an Eagle Scout. But, you see, he has some evidence backing him up. He received ten thousand dollars in a wire transfer, and Randall Hennessey received twenty-five. How would Calderone have known that Hennessey received that exact amount of money, unless he was telling the truth?

"And to bring it full circle, the wired money to both men

came from the same shadow organization. Does that not give Calderone's story not only reasonable, but total credibility?

"And how did Mr. Barnett react to the incriminating Calderone testimony? We don't know, because he disappeared the next day; you heard the detective testify to that. Here are two hypotheses for what might have happened: One, he feared his involvement in the murders was about to be proven, so he ran. Or, two, his co-conspirators feared that if Barnett went down, he'd take them with him, so they eliminated him.

"Are those hypotheses not at least reasonable?

"Ladies and gentlemen, Martha Boyer has lived an exemplary life. She has never knowingly hurt anyone, and she has devoted decades to saving unwanted animals. She has inherited a substantial amount of money and yet has lived a thoroughly modest life.

"But that life has thrown huge obstacles and pain in her path. Her husband was murdered; she has an awful disease that will take her life; and now she has to go through this terrible ordeal.

"Let your logic guide you as to what is reasonable and what is not, and then do the right thing. Let Martha Boyer live out her days at home, a free and innocent woman."

When I get back to the defense table, Pups leans over to talk to me again. This time, I assume she's going to tell me I screwed up, but instead she says, "Not bad."

That is what is known as high praise.

Judge Chambers gives his charge to the jury, and I am pleased that he discusses the absence of Barnett and says that the panel is free to assign whatever inference to it that they want. I think I've already gotten that across; if I haven't, then the jury has to be composed of twelve potted plants.

But having the judge's stamp of approval certainly cannot hurt, and it will increase my confidence while waiting for the verdict. But if my past experiences with verdict waiting are any guide, that confidence will last almost until I get to my car.

**T**he wait for this particular verdict is unique, at least in my career.

Not entirely; I'm still a nervous wreck and indulge my verdict-watch superstitions. For example, I will only make right turns, never left. This makes perfect sense to me, because I want the jury to do what's right.

So if I want to go left, I'll make three right turns to get me going in the desired direction. When I'm in my car, that's not such a big deal, and not noticeable. When I'm walking, I essentially make a 270-degree twirl, and people watching me generally assume I'm a lunatic and keep their distance.

I'll only eat certain kinds of foods, watch certain TV shows, take Tara and Sebastian for walks down certain streets. I have reasons for all of these things, but it would take too long, and they are too stupid, for me to list them here. Intellectually, I know what I'm doing, or not doing, has no influence on the jurors' actions, but just in case . . .

For all these reasons, I get nothing whatsoever of consequence accomplished during a verdict watch; I don't even try.

But, like I said, this time has to be different. Because if by some chance we win, then we have another trial following right on its heels. So I have to be productive, even though it does not come remotely naturally.

I meet Sam and Hike at the office to get an update. I also call Edna and ask her to come in, which comes as an unwelcome surprise to her. She naturally assumed that her work ended with the end of the trial, and the fact that her assumption was wrong is clearly jarring to her.

"We don't have another client, do we?" she asks, and seems somewhat reassured when I tell her we do not.

Sam has gone through Weisler's settlement offer, which, of course, will only be filed if Pups is acquitted by the criminal jury.

"I've gone through all the land holdings that he is proposing his client get, and the only one that rings a bell is still the South Dakota land that could possibly get the pipeline. If the other pieces have any potential value, I can't find it."

"Forget the pipeline situation for a moment. In terms of overall value, is his offer fair?"

"That's not for me to judge," Sam says. "But what he's asking for is probably 45 percent of the total value of the estate."

That comment tends to confirm my belief that there is something hidden here. I ask Hike what he thinks; until now, he has done nothing but cringe in fear that I am actually going to ask him to go to South Dakota.

He says, "I don't know how you could lay pipe on that

land. I looked at weather dot com; you know what the temperature is there today? Wind chill is minus eleven. Eyeballs freeze in that weather."

"So the people of South Dakota walk around bumping into things?"

He shakes his head. "No, their eyeballs are used to it and have adjusted. Someone from here—like me, for instance—wouldn't have a chance."

"Hike, you don't have to go there. Now what do you think?"

"Then the answer is in South Dakota."

Since Sam and Hike have placed a value on each piece of land, I construct a counteroffer. I redivide the land, giving Weisler 50 percent of the value, which is more than he asked for. But in this counterproposal, the South Dakota land stays with Pups. If he turns it down, it will be obvious to me that the South Dakota land is the key.

I have Edna type it up with the disclaimer that it is not binding and is subject to Martha's approval. Obviously, it is also subject to her being acquitted, since that is the only reason a civil suit would be filed.

We send it to him electronically, and then I call Walter Tillman to ask him to assist me on the civil trial should one be necessary. He knows much more about civil law than I do; between my criminal experience and knowledge of this case and his civil training, we would make a formidable team.

"Sure," he says. "Glad to help in any way I can." Then, "You think the civil suit will happen?"

It's his not-so-roundabout way of asking me what I think

the verdict will be in the criminal trial. "I don't know," I say. "I never know. I got a settlement offer from Weisler."

"And?"

"I sent him a counteroffer."

"Will Pups settle?" he asks, with obvious surprise.

"I haven't talked to her about it yet. It might be in her best interest, to put this all behind her. And the settlement would be sealed; no one would think she was a murderer. But it would mean less money for the rescue groups."

"You want me to talk to her?" he asks.

"Maybe. Let me broach it with her and see where we stand."

I get off the phone feeling a little better. If I have to go through a civil trial, Walter will be a major asset.

But first we have to hear from our jury.

**P**ups achieves a first among all my clients. She doesn't ask me if I think we're going to win. I've come to the jail to discuss the settlement offer, and I expected that to be her first question.

Wrong. Her first question is, "How is Puddles doing?"

"Willie says she's doing great. Micaela is still coming to visit her at the foundation, and she's got the reverse pet down pat."

She nods. "Good. What are you doing here?"

"Hank Boyer has made an offer to avoid a civil suit." I don't mention that if she's convicted he'll get it all anyway; she already knows that.

"Yeah?" is her noncommittal response.

I nod. "Yes."

"Is it a fair offer?"

I shrug. "I'm not sure. On its face it is, but I think there could be some hidden value on the land that we don't know about that is driving this." I pause and then plunge ahead. "It could be behind the murders as well."

"What the hell does that mean?"

"It means if Jake or you had sold some of the land, the people behind this might have gotten what they wanted."

"And Hank is part of this?"

"I don't see how, but I also don't see any other way the bad guys can profit."

She thinks about this for a while but doesn't say anything. I have no idea what is going through her mind. Finally, she says, "No settlement. If Jake didn't want him to get anything, then I don't either."

"That's what I thought you'd say. But with your permission, or even without it, I'm going to keep the discussions going."

"Why?" she asks.

"I'm trying to draw them out, to find out what's important to them and what isn't."

She nods. "OK. I trust you."

It feels good to hear her say that; somehow when Pups gives a compliment, it has more impact than when other people do.

"Let me ask you a question," I say. "How come you haven't asked me whether I think we're going to win or lose?"

She shrugs. "Would it change anything if I did?"

"No."

"There's your answer."

I'm about to get up and leave when there is a knock on the door, and it opens. A guard is standing in the doorway with a very scary message.

"They want you in the courtroom," he says to Pups.

Pups takes the news much more calmly than I do. She needs to be escorted by law enforcement, so I leave and will meet her there. I call Hike and tell him the news, and he'll meet us there as well.

If it's a verdict, then I think it's bad news. I've instinctively felt that our chances in this one increase the longer the jury takes. Of course, if they took a month before reaching a verdict, I would think that was bad news as well. I'm a verdict-half-empty kind of guy.

I see Tressel when I walk in, and he comes over to me. "No verdict," he says. "The jury has a message for the judge."

In all such cases, the key players, including the defendant, must be present. It could be anything from a question about evidence to declaring themselves hung. We won't know until we know.

And we know soon enough. Chambers brings in the jury, and the foreman quickly tells him that they collectively believe they are deadlocked and are very unlikely to resolve it and come to a verdict.

Chambers will have none of it; he tells the foreman that they need to go back and try again and work hard to make it happen. There is no hint of where the jury stands, whether the majority is in favor of an acquittal or a conviction.

In a normal case, the defense is usually happy with a situation like this, but, once again, this case is not normal. Pups just doesn't have that much time left, so the time needed to schedule and hold a retrial essentially means life in prison for her.

The guards escort her back to the prison, and I check my

cell phone once I get out of court. There's a message from Weisler, asking me to call him, so I do.

"We're getting close," he says. "I just need one more thing to sell it to my client, a slight reshuffling of the land distribution."

"What's that?" I ask, though I have no doubt what it will be.

"The South Dakota land is important to him. That's his home state; it's where he wants to spend the rest of his life. That land would be perfect. We'd be willing to trade more than fair value."

"I'll bet you would," is what I'm thinking. What I say is, "I've got another idea; let's make it all or nothing and try the case."

**T**he civil suit is filed twenty-four hours after my conversation with Weisler.

In lawsuit land, that qualifies as warp speed, but it doesn't surprise me. They clearly have no great reason to wait, since we're not going to settle. Civil cases also involve discovery depositions, and they want to be able to question Pups under oath before her disease claims her.

If Pups is convicted, they can and will just withdraw the suit and set about getting her estate. At that point, she will no longer own it anyway, since she cannot inherit Jake's estate if she has been found criminally to have murdered him.

In any event, I want to get a jump on the opposition by filing a deposition notice to interview Hank Boyer before they can interview Pups. I instruct Hike to file the notice with Weisler. I doubt they'll try to delay; they seem to be in something of a hurry.

I'm still nervously awaiting the jury's decision in the criminal case, but I'm pessimistic. In football, they say that when a quarterback throws a pass, three things can happen, and two of them are bad. There can be an incompletion, an interception, or a completion—the single good outcome.

We are facing a similar situation in this deliberation. Three things can happen, and two of them are bad. While an acquittal would obviously be positive, the other two possible outcomes, a conviction or a hung jury, are both bad. If the jury is hung, then all Tressel has to do is announce that he will retry the case, and Pups will essentially be confined to prison for the rest of her brief life.

There is no way to know what the jury's breakdown was when they told Judge Chambers that they couldn't reach a verdict. Based on my history of instinctively reading juries, I can confidently say that in the jury's vote so far, we are either ahead, behind, or tied.

In other words, I don't have a clue.

Another twenty-four hours pass, and I'm about to go off the deep end. I'm spending the days sitting on my couch, trying to divert myself by watching every sporting event on television. And with all the sports channels, there is no sporting event that isn't on television.

Every time the phone rings, I jump off the couch to get it. I finally come up with a new plan; I bring the phone onto the couch with me. I'm watching a nationally televised spelling bee when Sam calls.

"That South Dakota bill finally came out of committee," he says. "The news just broke."

"They chose the route through Pups's land," I say, more as a statement than a question. If they chose otherwise, them I'm at square 1.

"Yup," he says. "Locals are very surprised; there was another route that everybody expected."

"So what reason did they give for choosing this one?" I ask.

"No one is saying on the record, at least not so far. Just a lot of environmental stuff, best for the people of South Dakota, blah, blah, blah. Apparently, a state senator named Ridgeway is the head of the committee, and he pushed it through."

"So it's a done deal?" I ask.

"Seems like it."

I hang up and call Nolan Weisler. He had called me about timing for the depositions, and we've traded calls since. "Looks like Jake's dream home won't work out," I say. "They're going to be laying pipeline there."

He knows exactly what I'm saying and doesn't seem at all embarrassed by it. "You can't blame me for doing my homework."

The truth is that I can't. "How did you know that would be the route they would choose?"

"I didn't," he said. "But there was always that chance, and the rest of the land in the estate is pretty much a waste of time."

We change the subject to the timing of the civil depositions, which of course are subject to the criminal jury's verdict. "You think the jury will be hung?" he asks.

"Or not."

If they are hung, the civil suit will move forward, so we set up the first deposition, that of Hank Boyer, for next week. If Pups gets convicted in the meantime, we'll just cancel it.

I head back to my couch, just in time to see a snotty little brat misspell "potpourri." He uses one *r*; it would be embarrassing for him to lose like this in front of a national television audience, except for the fact that I have to be the only dope who is tuned in.

Now another snotty little brat steps to the podium, needing to spell one more word to be declared the winner. Unfortunately, the phone rings again. Even more unfortunately, the caller ID says that the call is coming from the courthouse.

It's Rita Gordon. "It's showtime, Andy. The judge wants you down at the courthouse."

"Has the jury come back?" I ask.

"This does involve the jury," she says, obviously guarded.

"Is there a verdict?"

"Andy, you know I can't tell you that. The judge would kill me. We have rules."

"Rules, shmules," I say.

"Rules, shmules? Is that the best you've got?"

"I become less eloquent the more nervous I get. Come on, Rita. We'll all know in an hour; I can keep your secret that long."

"OK," she says. "But if you tell anyone, I'll hunt you down and kill you like the lawyer dog you are."

"I can live with that."

"Andy, there's a verdict."

**B**y the time I get to the courthouse, most of the players are in place.

Tressel and his team are there, as is Hike. The gallery is half full, and the rest of the seats are filling rapidly. Laurie has come with me, and she takes her seat behind the defense table. We have a little preverdict ritual in which she doesn't wish me luck but squeezes my hand, and she reaches over and does that.

Pups is brought in; she's coughing and not looking well. But she gathers herself and smiles when she sits down next to me. "What is it this time?"

I think I can safely tell her without getting Rita in trouble; I doubt that Pups is going to scream out the fact that there's a verdict. "This is it," I say, and she knows what I mean.

Judge Chambers comes in and announces that the jury has communicated to him that they have, in fact, reached a verdict. He then mouths the obligatory drivel about how everyone must maintain decorum after the verdict is announced, though the next time someone is punished for violating the decorum edict will be the first.

The jury is brought into the room. I don't subscribe to the theory that it's bad if the jury doesn't look at me or good if they do. In this case, they don't look at either the defense or the prosecution, but they all look down in a seemingly common fascination with their own shoes.

Judge Chambers, to his credit, doesn't drag this out. As soon as the jury is seated, he asks the foreman if they have reached a verdict, and the foreman confirms that they have. Chambers directs the bailiff to retrieve the verdict form and bring it to him, and the bailiff does so.

Chambers glances at it in what seems to be a weirdly disinterested manner, as if he's saying that all he cares about is conducting a fair trial; it doesn't matter who wins or loses. It's possible that I'm reading too much into this; it's also possible that my head is going to explode.

Chambers hands it to the court clerk and asks Pups to stand. She does so, and Hike and I stand as well. She seems a little shaky; the stress of what she has gone through has to have taken its toll. I put my arm around her shoulder as Chambers asks the clerk to read the verdict out loud.

"In the matter of *New Jersey vs. Martha Boyer,* as relating to count one, the homicide of Mr. Jake Boyer, we the jury find the defendant, Martha Boyer, not guilty of murder in the first degree."

The gallery erupts enough to stop the clerk from reading, and Chambers has to admonish them and gavel the place back to silence. In most cases, I would be totally relieved, but this case is not the typical one. The Hennessey murder is where the prosecution had the most evidence; the jury could easily have compromised by finding Pups guilty of that one and not guilty of the others.

The clerk continues to read. "In the matter of *New Jersey vs. Martha Boyer,* as relating to count two, the homicide of Mr. Raymond Parker, we the jury find the defendant, Martha Boyer, not guilty of murder in the first degree."

That is no surprise; it would be impossible to find her not guilty of killing Jake but guilty of killing Little Tiny. Obviously, the shooter was the same in both cases.

I gird myself for the next one.

"In the matter of *New Jersey vs. Martha Boyer,* as relating to count three, the homicide of Mr. Randall Hennessey, we the jury find the defendant, Martha Boyer, not guilty of murder in the first degree."

Relief washes over me; if there is a better feeling in the world, I don't know what it is. I take my hand off of Pups's shoulder and cast a quick glance at a very happy Laurie. I then turn back to Pups and am surprised to see that she is not there, and instead I am looking at Hike.

That's because Pups is lying on the floor.

According to the doctor, Pups hadn't been taking her heart medication.

The result was the same supraventricular thing that sent her to the hospital last time, once again brought on by high stress. They took her to the hospital, and, as before, medication got her feeling better in thirty-six hours.

I've come to see her, and I start by admonishing her for not taking the meds. "Mind your own business," she says. Pups is not great at being admonished.

"You're my client, so you're my business," I say. "Take the damn meds."

"They make me dizzy," she says.

"Not taking them makes you unconscious," I point out. "And you need to be strong; we have another trial coming up."

"Do I have to be there?"

"Not the whole time. But you have to give a deposition and then testify. It will take a lot of energy and focus. Unless you want to settle."

She shakes her head. "No chance."

"There's been a development in South Dakota regarding your property. It could be worth a fortune."

She nods. "Good. More money for the rescue groups."

"OK. Whenever I win a case, we have a victory party at Charlie's. You up to it when you get out of here? Would you rather wait until after the civil case wraps up?"

"Hey, we won, so we party," she says. "We can party again when we win the next round."

"Next round is tougher."

"Why? If I'm innocent once, I'll be innocent again."

"I told you already. Different standard of guilt, a much lower bar for them to get over. It also doesn't have to be unanimous. The criminal jury had a tough time with this one, which may not bode well for the civil case."

She doesn't want to hear about it, so I ask whom she wants me to invite to the party.

"Whoever you want," she says. "I'll invite my friends, and give me Willie Miller's phone number."

"I can invite Willie," I say.

"Just give me the number."

It's a strange request. "Why?"

"You writing a book?" she asks. "Or is his number a state secret?"

I give her Willie's number, and we set the party for tomorrow at seven PM, provided that she's released from the hospital on schedule.

Preparing to try the civil case will not be nearly as difficult or intensive as doing so for the criminal case. I'm going to be covering the same ground, and I already have a total command of the facts. I'll also have Hike with me, as well as Walter Tillman to help with the nuances of civil versus criminal.

We should be fine. It doesn't mean we'll win, but we'll do a good job. I have to admit I'm feeling confident.

As to the big picture, I still don't know what Barnett and his accomplices hoped to gain. Maybe they were taken by surprise by Hank's entry into the picture; it could have foiled some hidden plan they had.

The shooter is still out there; I'm sure of that. It could mean that Hank is in some physical jeopardy. If they get rid of him, maybe they can go back to their original plan. I think I'll mention this to Nolan Weisler. I want his client to lose the case; I don't want him to die.

I head back to work, and when I get to my second-floor office, I find that the door is ajar. I should take that as an ominous sign, but I'm not thinking quickly enough, and I find myself staring at Big Tiny Parker and two of his large friends.

"How did you get in here?" I ask.

"We broke the lock," he says, as if that's the most normal thing in the world.

"Why?"

"Because we didn't want to stand in the hall," Big Tiny says.

This is the first time I've been around him without Marcus present, and I can't say I like this new arrangement. "What do you want?"

"Who killed my brother?" he asks.

"I don't know yet."

"That ain't good enough. The case is over."

I shake my head. "The trial is over. The case is not over."

"You think you can screw around with me?" he asks.

I'm getting more than a little nervous. "Look, a guy named Barnett ordered the hit; I'm sure of that. I exposed him, and he's gone. And I think it's a good bet that he's dead. But I don't know yet who the shooter is. I'm doing my best."

"Maybe you should be watching out for your own ass," he says, and they walk out of the office. It is an abrupt way to end our little meeting, and his last line was a bit cryptic. Was he threatening me, or warning me to watch out for the shooter?

I'm unsure, and I'm also unnerved.

**A**s we always do for our victory parties, we take over the second floor of Charlie's.

Laurie and I got a sitter for Ricky, but she's a little late arriving, so we don't get to the party until ten minutes after it started. Willie and Sondra are there, as is Hike, Sam, Edna, Marcus, Walter Tillman, and Vince. Vince really had nothing to do with the trial, but the concept of free food and beer makes him feel like one of the team.

Pups is there, as are quite a few of her friends, so there are maybe thirty people in all. Pups is holding court in one corner of the room, sitting in a chair and greeting everyone. She looks weak but happy.

I have no doubt that one of the main reasons for her happiness is the presence of the only nonhuman in the room. Her dog, Puddles, sits on her lap. Willie obviously brought Puddles, which is why Pups wanted his number. I've never seen a dog in Charlie's before, and I'm sure it must violate some ordinance. I'm also sure that Pups was not about to be denied.

David Rosenfelt

When Pups sees me, she clanks her glass to gain everyone's attention. "Here he is," she proclaims, "the greatest lawyer in the history of the world."

While I'm not about to quarrel with her assessment, the comment was very un-Pups-like. I don't see a drink in her hand, so it can't be that she's drunk. But it is rather strange.

The party settles in, and everyone seems to be having fun. While the specter of the civil trial hangs over me, nobody else except Walter and Hike seems to be aware of it. In their minds, the criminal trial was the be-all and end-all, and it has ended in a huge triumph.

Walter, Hike, and I hold a brief conversation about what lies ahead, and Hike asks if Pups might reconsider settling. Walter laughs at his lack of understanding of our client. "She will fight until the very end, and even longer," Walter says. "That is one tough lady."

"I think we're going to win," I say. "We'll nail them with the same things we used at trial, and now we can point to the land situation in South Dakota. We've got a lot of weapons. Plus, we have a terminally ill woman trying to give her money to save animals versus a gold-digging kid who never gave his father the time of day."

"I like your style," Walter says. "And you throw a great party."

Laurie is talking to Pups, so I start walking over there. As I'm doing so, I see the door open and three people come in. It is Micaela Reasoner, the young girl who took such a liking to Puddles, and two adults that I assume are her parents. Either Willie or Pups must have invited them.

Micaela brightens up when she sees Puddles sitting in Pups's lap. She runs over and starts petting and hugging her. Her parents stand there, smiling.

"Are you Micaela?" asks Pups.

She nods but keeps petting. "Yup."

"Did you learn the reverse pet?"

"I sure did," she says, demonstrating it. "Puddles loves it."

"I know," says Pups. "You do it very well."

"Is Puddles your dog?" Micaela asks.

"She was."

"Not anymore?"

Pups shakes her head. "No, now she's your dog. Take very good care of her." Pups gives Puddles a kiss on the head and then hands her to Micaela.

"What are you doing?" Micaela asks. "What do you mean?"

"Don't you want her?"

"Are you kidding?" she says, almost shrieking, and holding Puddles to her chest. "I want her more than anything in the world!" Then she turns to her mother and says, "Mom?"

Micaela's mother nods, laughs, and cries all at the same time. Pups obviously must have cleared it with her in advance. Laurie's crying as well, and I'm coming damn close.

The only one not crying is Pups, and I don't know how she isn't. I can't imagine the pain she is feeling at giving up her dog. But she knows she is dying, and what she is doing is an amazingly selfless act.

"Merry Christmas," Pups says.

Micaela looks a little confused. "But Christmas is over."

Pups smiles. "It doesn't have to be."

Micaela gives Pups a hug, and her parents introduce themselves and thank her. Then Puddles goes off with her new family, and, once they're gone, Pups says, "Who do you have to know to get a drink around here?"

**T**hat was an incredible thing she did," Laurie says in the car on the way home from the party. "She made sure that dog will be loved long after she is gone."

I nod. "She's a terrific lady."

Laurie looks over at me. "What's wrong?"

"I just wish she didn't have to go through all this legal garbage."

"You're doing all you can, which has been quite a bit."

I can feel that she's staring at me, and I ask her why.

"Don't walk the dogs for too long tonight," she says.

If she's implying what I think she's implying, I'll take the dogs on a run instead of a walk, to get it finished faster.

We get home, and while Laurie is paying the babysitter, I grab the leashes and am out the door with Tara and Sebastian. We head for Eastside Park, but we'll take a shorter route than usual. I don't tell them why; I'm too ashamed.

They love these walks, and I love to watch them loving them. And while I completely admire what Pups did, I don't think I could give them up until they were lowering me into the ground.

It's a cold, quiet night, and the only sound I hear is my shoes and their paws, crunching into the snow. In a typical winter, the snow never leaves once it falls on this grass; the park is never crowded so it just lies there, blanketing the ground and remaining mostly white. Just like Bing Crosby didn't remember it.

We're near the old and now empty zoo, which was never much to speak of and only has a few small buildings. I'm about to turn around and head back home when Tara freezes and then turns to the left. She must see something, probably a squirrel. During the daytime, I let her chase squirrels because I know she could never catch them and wouldn't know what to do with one if she did.

But there's no time for that tonight. "Come on, girl; let's go home."

But she doesn't move; she's still intent on whatever she senses. And then she does something that sends a chill through me, which has nothing to do with the temperature outside.

She growls.

Tara simply does not growl. I've never heard her do it, not once. I look in the direction she's pointing, and it's dark, but I think I see movement.

It's no squirrel.

I'm not sure what to do. My two choices are to run or hide. I'm not going to leave the dogs behind, so running is out. It's dark enough that I may be able to stay out of sight. I wish I hadn't left my damn phone at home.

There's a small building that is open. It's hard to see in the dark, but I think it's a deserted refreshment stand. I quietly take Tara and Sebastian in there, tie their leashes together, and tie the other end around a pole. They should be safe in here.

"Come on out, Carpenter. Nice and slow."

It's not a voice I'm familiar with and is maybe the scariest I've ever heard. It's a confident voice; it's the voice of somebody who knows that they've won.

I've done the worst thing possible; I've led us into a dead end. Literally and figuratively.

I don't know what to do, so I do nothing. And then I hear a sound scarier than the voice. It's a gunshot, and the bullet seems to ricochet off the wall to the left. He can't see us, which is a positive. But we're in a small area, and eventually he will be unable to miss.

I can't stay here; it would be just waiting to die. I move Tara and Sebastian behind a table and tie them up there; it's as safe as I can make it. I edge toward the door. In the darkness maybe I can get out without him seeing me. I don't for a second believe it's possible, but I can't come up with anything better.

I hear another gunshot, but even though I flinch and recoil, it doesn't seem to have been aimed at the building. Then I hear some other noises outside. I can't tell what they are. There's some movement, and I think I hear a voice. I don't know what is going on, and I don't want to wait around to find out. As I reach the door, I'm about to run into the darkness, when suddenly it's not dark anymore.

There's a beam of light, and it's shined on me, focused in on my chest. I am about to die.

I look ahead; it's very hard to get my eyes to adjust. But I can tell there's more than one person there, maybe three or four. And they are large.

"Come on out. You're OK," says a voice, but this is a different voice than before. It's one I recognize.

Slowly my eyes adjust, and I'm looking at Big Tiny Parker and two of his guys. There's a fourth person there, but he's lying on the ground at their feet.

"This is the guy that killed my brother," Big Tiny says. It's not a question; it's a statement of fact.

I look at the person on the ground; he's holding his shoulder and is definitely alive. "I think it is," I say. Conspiracies like this one generally try to limit the participants, so as to limit the risk of exposure. It's therefore unlikely that they would have doled out the violence to a number of practitioners.

I ask Big Tiny, "You were following me?"

"Yeah. I told you to watch your ass," he says. "So we watched it for you. And now we got what we want."

"You need to let the police handle this," I say. "There's a lot we can find out."

"No," Big Tiny says, in a tone that doesn't sound like he's inclined to open negotiations. "That's not the way this works."

"I can't let you take him," I say.

"Then you're going to die with him. You got one chance to get out of here, and you'd better take it now."

I go back inside and untie Tara and Sebastian. My choice is pretty simple. I can take them home and live or stay and die defending a murderer.

Heading home.

make the decision on the way home.

I am not going to tell anyone what has happened. Nothing good can come of it, and I don't want to be a part of the bad that will follow.

Of course, Laurie is not anyone. I can't think of anything I wouldn't share with her, so when she asks me what took so long on the walk, I unload the whole story.

I do this despite knowing that she will be upset by it, and not just because I was almost killed. Laurie was a cop, a dedicated, outstanding cop, and she believes in the justice system. What Big Tiny did tonight was vigilante revenge, pure and simple.

"Oh, Andy . . . ," she says when I am almost finished with the story. She comes over and hugs me. It feels great, particularly since forty minutes ago I thought I'd never hug her again.

"I know you don't approve of what I did," I say. "But I had no choice. They would have killed me as well."

"I understand that," she says.

"And there's nothing we can do now. I have no evidence other than what I saw, and I don't even know the name of the shooter. I didn't even see his face."

"I know that," she says. "It's OK, Andy. I understand. I would have done the same thing. The shooter was going to die tonight no matter what you did."

I nod. "Yes, but there's something you should know about me."

She pulls back in surprise at my words and tone. "What is it?"

"The only thing I'm sorry about, and I mean the only thing, is that I never got to find out what that guy knew. It could have answered a lot of questions, and maybe even helped me in the civil case. Do you understand? Other than that, I don't have the slightest regret that he's dead."

"Andy . . ."

"Let me finish. He would have killed me, and I have no doubt he killed Jake Boyer and Randall Hennessey and Big Tiny's brother and probably David Barnett. I understand Big Tiny needing revenge, and I'm fine with it. I think, if I had to, I could have pulled the trigger myself."

"I understand," she says. "And here's what you should know about me. I think you did the absolute right thing, and I would trade a thousand killers like that for one of you. I also respect your right to let it end right here and now. But I'm sorry that guy is dead, no matter who or what he was, because I do not approve of murder, in any form or circumstance."

I nod. "You say tomayto, and I say tomahto. You say potayto, and I say potahto."

She doesn't want to laugh, but she can't help herself. "You're a childish idiot."

I nod again. "I am aware of that."

**W**e're as ready for the civil case as we ever will be.

I've got a lot of witnesses lined up, who I think will make a compelling case. Included in that group are the police officers who testified at the first trial. The difference is that they believe the jury verdict was correct, and now they will be testifying for us rather than against us.

There is still no sign of David Barnett. I don't think there is a chance in hell that he is still alive or that his body is going to be found. I think the guy in the park took care of that, not realizing that he was soon going to follow Barnett into oblivion.

We start the deposition process tomorrow, and Hank Boyer is the first witness. Even though he is the plaintiff, his testimony is not particularly important. This trial is to determine whether Martha Boyer is civilly responsible for the death of her husband, and Hank knows nothing about that. He didn't even know his father was dead until I told him when I was in Deadwood.

All I'm going to try to get on the record with Hank's testimony is his total estrangement from his father. I don't want the jury to feel sorry for him at trial; he is not the mourning son, and I don't want him to pretend to be.

The only thing still nagging at me is the question of how the bad guys hoped to get Jake and Martha's estate. If Hank is part of the conspiracy, he went about it in a strange way, waiting for eighteen months and my intervention before doing anything. The conspirators could have set Martha up for Jake's murder back then; I don't know what they, or Jake, had to gain by waiting.

But today is Sunday, and I'm taking the day off from any thoughts of work. Ricky and I are going into New York City, to an event at the Michelangelo Hotel, on Fifty-First.

It turns out that Pups has two already-paid-for season tickets to the Mets games for the upcoming season. She and Jake had them for years, long before Citi Field was built and the Mets were playing at Shea Stadium. She has given them to me as a thank-you gift for representing her.

I looked at the seating chart and was shocked to see that they are in the first row behind the dugout, quite literally the best seats in the stadium. They're so good and so expensive that along with the seats comes a membership in the Mets Booster Club.

There's no end to the things about Pups that I didn't know.

So today we're attending a booster luncheon for the Mets, sort of a send-off before they go to spring training. She said that some of the Mets players are always there, and they will sign autographs and talk to the kids. Ricky is wildly excited about it, while his cool father is pretending not to be.

The luncheon is for maybe 150 people, and we get seats near the front. The manager and three players are there, and each talk about how excited they are for the upcoming season, blah, blah, blah.

It's not exciting stuff, but Ricky is eating it up, and I enjoy watching him. I feel pretty confident he will be a sports degenerate, like his father.

What he's really looking forward to is the autograph session, which will take place at the end of the speeches and lunch. When that time finally comes, we all go into an adjacent room, where four tables are set up. One is for the manager, and the other three are for the players. People line up at a table to get autographs and a few words with their heroes, and Ricky has brought six baseballs to be signed.

One of Ricky's favorite players happens to be here today. The Mets have great young pitching, and one of those pitchers is named Steven Matz. He's the only left-hander in the starting staff, and he's got all the potential in the world.

So Ricky and I line up at Steven Matz's table, and we're fourth in line. When we get to the front, Matz couldn't be nicer. He asks Ricky's name, where he goes to school, what position he plays, etcetera, and, all in all, makes Ricky feel like a million dollars.

Finally, Matz asks Ricky what he wants signed, and he hands him two baseballs.

Matz takes a pen and signs the first one, and in the process tells me everything I need to know about the murders of Jake Boyer, Little Tiny Parker, and Randall Hennessey.

**Y**esterday was a very busy day.

Starting the moment Ricky and I got home from the Mets luncheon, I began working the phones and preparing. Laurie pitched in, and we called everyone from the county coroner, Janet Carlson, to Pete Stanton, to FBI agent Cindy Spodek, our good friend.

I also had to call Pups, just to reconfirm something that she once said to me, and then I went back through some of the case documents, checking a couple of things that I had overlooked before. But everything has fallen into place as I expected, thanks to Mets pitcher Steven Matz.

As agreed on earlier, we are holding the deposition at the office of Nolan Weisler, Hank Boyer's attorney. I was fine with that; it's a lot nicer than my office, and you don't have to walk past a fruit stand and up a flight of stairs.

Weisler seemed surprised when I called him yesterday and told him that we'd be bringing six instead of three people. "We're going for quantity rather than quality," I said.

The three members of our team on the legal side, Hike,

Walter Tillman, and me, arrive separately. The other three people I invited are Pete Stanton and two uniformed police officers of his choosing. They arrive five minutes before the ten AM start time for the deposition.

On the other side of the table are Hank Boyer, Nolan Weisler, another attorney from his office, and a court reporter who will take down everything that is said. She will also administer the oath to Hank.

Both Hank and Weisler seem surprised by the police presence, but they don't ask why they are there, nor would I tell them if they did. I have a right to bring whomever I want to sit in on the deposition.

Weisler, Walter, and I have decided that we are going to split up the witnesses, each of us doing certain depositions, in order to ease the workload. I had said, however, that for this first one, we should all be present, even though I would be asking the actual questions.

It's not going to take long.

Once we're settled, I read into the record for the court reporter the names of those in attendance. Then I start the questioning, saying to Hank, "Please state your name for the record."

"Hank Boyer," he says.

"Sorry," I say, "but it's a legal proceeding, so we need your real full name."

"Oh. Henry Alan Boyer."

"Please have the record show that I have asked the witness his name twice, and he has refused to provide it."

Weisler interrupts. "What's going on here? He told you his real name."

"No, he didn't. He said Henry Boyer. His real name is Floyd Reynolds."

Weisler looks bewildered, but Hank Boyer, real name Floyd Reynolds, looks like he's been shot by a Taser.

"What the hell is going on here?" Weisler asks, and then says to the court reporter, "We're off the record now."

Pete Stanton says, "No, we stay on the record."

"Thanks, Pete," I say, and I start reading from a document. "Floyd Reynolds: thirty-seven years old; born Cedar Rapids, Iowa; two felony convictions, one for fraud and one for breaking and entering. Served a total of three years and four months in prison on the two convictions." I look up and add, "Which is nothing compared to the time he's about to serve for conspiracy to commit murder."

Hank/Floyd finally snaps out of his stunned mode and stands up. "Murder? What the hell is going on here?"

The thing is, the really important thing, is that he doesn't yell the question at me. He yells it at Walter Tillman.

As I knew he would.

"Sit down," Walter says. "We need to take a break here."

"This is bullshit. You told me nothing could go wrong."

"Shut up," Walter says, obviously worried.

Hank/Floyd points to Walter. "He's your murderer, not me. I was just playing a role for money. Like acting—that's what he said."

Pete stands and reads Hank/Floyd his rights, placing him under arrest. Then he turns to Walter and smiles, "Your turn is coming real soon."

**Y**ou knew Tillman was bad?" Hike asks as we leave Weisler's office.

Pete and the other two officers have left with Hank/Floyd, and Tillman went wherever people go when they know they're in deep shit. I doubt he would try to run; he's not the hunted-fugitive type. He's a lawyer; he'll more likely opt to fight it out on his home field, in court.

As we were leaving, Weisler had come up to me and said, "I hope you know I had no knowledge of this."

"Actually, I don't know either way," I said. "And that's not my problem anymore."

But back to Hike's question about my awareness of Tillman's role in the conspiracy. "I did," I say. "I realized it yesterday at the Mets booster luncheon."

"What the hell are you talking about?"

"Steven Matz was there; he's a left-handed pitcher. He's really good, and when he signed Ricky's baseball with his left hand, it clicked in my mind."

"What did?"

"A while back, I asked Pups what she knew about Jake's son. She knew very little, but she mentioned that Jake had hoped that one day he would become another Jerry Koosman. Jerry Koosman was a left-hander."

"Maybe Jake just picked a good pitcher's name; maybe he wasn't thinking about right and left."

"No chance. If you were a real Mets fan, you'd know what I mean. Tom Seaver was on that team, and he was a Hall of Famer, much better than Koosman. If Jake was just looking for a Mets pitcher, he would have said Seaver. But Koosman was a lefty, and Seaver a righty. If he went out of his way to say that his son would become a Koosman, that son had to be a lefty."

Hike shakes his head at this, maybe because he never watches baseball. "How did you know this Floyd guy wasn't left-handed as well?"

"Because he dealt blackjack to me in Deadwood. He used a single deck, and he held the cards in his left hand, and dealt them out with his right. Only a right-hander would do it that way."

"So that's how you knew this guy wasn't really Hank. But you still haven't answered my question. How did you know Tillman was in on it?"

"Tillman gave me the picture of Hank, which I took to Deadwood with me. He said he got it from Jake when he was preparing the will, but it was a picture of Floyd. There's no way that Jake would have given him that."

"That's it?"

I shake my head. "No. Tillman handled their money. He

sent me a check for my fee from their account; Pups didn't have to sign it."

"So?"

"So that's how Devereux got the fifty grand: Tillman secretly sent it from Jake's account. She never had an affair with him. Remind me to tell Pete to arrest her for perjury."

"So Tillman was right in the middle all along. He was playing both sides."

"Right. That's why they didn't frame Pups eighteen months ago. The offers were coming from Barnett through Tillman. Tillman figured she would agree to sell land, whereas Jake never would. But she refused each time, for no reason other than she was honoring what Jake would have wanted. Pups can be a bit stubborn, so they needed to get to her estate this way."

"So they always had the fake Hank in their back pocket?"

I nod. "Yes; this was always their plan B. These guys were careful, and they were smart. They cast Floyd in this role a long time ago."

"Not bad," Hike says. "Who did the shooting?"

I almost say, "The guy in the park. The one Big Tiny killed." But instead I go with, "I don't have any idea."

**P**ups's funeral was today. She had one last surprise up her sleeve.

There had to be five hundred people there. And I always thought she was a hermit. Pups made a lot of friends in a life well lived.

She lived for six weeks after the day of the aborted deposition. The case has exploded since then, thanks to Big Tiny Parker. He sent me the shooter's phone with an anonymous note saying that the owner of the phone was dead and that he had been the killer of, among others, Little Tiny Parker.

There was a treasure trove of information on the phone, whose deceased owner went by the name Caffey. It propelled the investigation from here to South Dakota and back. Tillman was arrested for murder, and a state senator named Ridgeway was found to be the victim of blackmail because of a secret sex tape. His role was to make sure the pipeline went through Jake's land. It's uncertain what will be done to him, either by the justice system or by his wife.

Nolan Weisler is in the clear; he seems not to have had

any idea what was going on around him. Some recovered e-mails from Caffey indicate that the real Hank was a day laborer who was one of Caffey's first victims, but there is no way to know where that happened or where his body is buried.

I told Pups almost all of this, and she seemed most happy that people would know that Jake never had that affair. The only thing I didn't tell her about was Tillman's involvement. She was close to him, and she and Jake trusted him. Then I started to feel like I owed her all the truth, so about a week ago I went to see her. It turned out that it would be for the last time.

She was obviously not doing well, so I didn't want to bother her for too long. I quickly told her about Tillman's role in all of it and his arrest.

She was sort of dazed, and I didn't know whether she understood me. She shook her head slightly, and then all she said in response was one word:

"Lawyers."

And then she smiled.